When Day

Day
Day
Night
Night

Meets Night

WHEN DAY

Meets NIGHT

by

Ramadhan

Published by *UPSTREAM PUBLICATIONS*
A division of A&B PUBLISHERS GROUP
1000 Atlantic Ave.
Brooklyn, NY 11238
(718) 783-7808

ISBN 1-886433-35-6

COVER ILLUSTRATION: © *Andre Harriss*
TYPESETTING & INTERIOR DESIGN: *Industrial Fonts & Graphix*

Manufactured & Printed in Canada
01 02 03 04 05 06   10 9 8 7 6 5 4 3 2 1

DEDICATION

This book is dedicated to my grandfather Russell Bassett Sr. and my uncle Earnest Bassett two men who were the backbone of our family.

I would also like to acknowledge my parents, and my brother and sister. Also the Benton family as well as everyone that held me down when I was blazin' my pen. (Speedy, Breez)

THE DARK SIDE

Red The Jux Master

*M*y son wakes me up by sitting on my chest and playing with my nose. He's a mischievous seven-year-old just like I was, and if he's in here bothering me, then his mother must be preoccupied. I look to my left and day and night fight for position . . . Dusk is fully exposed as the reddish sky awakens all of the nocturnal creatures that inhabit this world. I change my focus to the top drawer of the dresser. I'm not sure how long my son's been here and he might have made a random search. It's all good; the paper I wedged along the edge of the drawer would have fallen if he made any unauthorized attempts at entry.

Tyriq is the spitting image of me: the light brown hair, light-brown copper skin, the hazel eyes and round face make us look like twins. But his smooth walk and semi-manipulative demeanor without a doubt lets niggas know that this is my seed. I send him on his way and make my way to the drawer that holds the powerful semi-natural substance that helps me make it through my nights. I remove the marijuana-filled cigar, which was half smoked last night, open the window and spark the scomas. I inhale deeply, allowing its potent power to fill my lungs and affect my mind. I inhale again this time holding the smoke in longer than before and slowly it begins to numb the pain, and distort the reality of this hell.

I finish my morning dosage and move to the hiding place of my blower. My loyal and trusted 45mm beretta, 15 in the clip one in head, built-in silencer and optional laser sighting attachment. It's loaded with subsonic bullets, grain 147. Those are the same bullets used by SWAT teams. Yo, I love this chic more than my son's mother, she's been with me through thick and thin, she's never turned on me and she saved my life a few times. My son's mother ain't did nothin' but piss me off.

I move to the bathroom to begin my hygienic ritual and there in the tub is a sickening sight. The naked water-covered body of my son's mother, she's the ugliest crab-ass bitch I've ever met. A lot of niggas don't understand why I hate her so much because she's really pretty. True, she's not a dime piece but she's far from busted. It's just that inside she's so twisted that it's distorted my view of her.

When we first met, I was in the early stages of my stick-up game and I was living carelessly. Clothes, jewels, rental cars every week, just spending money like it didn't matter. So of course she wanted to ride the money train with the rest of the local chics. At first she was just a shorty to knock off, then she became an addiction. On the flip, she ended up being a real trooper, she stayed with me through a lot of bullshit. She did my first bid with me; for a buck and half she came through with packages and visits. Then she got pregnant and everything changed 'cause my son changed my outlook on a few things. The stick-up game that used to be a reckless gun-slinging adventure became a calculated systematic art. I can't afford not to come home one night; I can't afford to be laid out with two to the dome. The older he got the less chances I took and now that he's turning into me, I want to be removed from this land of blood with no glory.

I grew but she didn't. She wanted that reckless life back, but she loves us too much to leave us, and now she hates me for my growth. She's made me hate her 'cause she continues to disrespect herself in public by maintaining groupie status to any cat around the way with a little hustlin' money. She talks about me like a dog every chance she gets and no matter what I say, she stays flippin' on me for dumb shit one of her chicken-head friends told her. At least once a week she comes to me with some bullshit about how so and so said I was fuckin' whoever. She's a 100% official U.S.D.A.-approved drama queen. She's addicted to being in the middle of some off-the-wall shit and if it's nowhere to be found she'll make some. At one time I had repeatedly fallen victim and got caught up in her games but now I'm just here to make sure my little man is right. As soon as everything falls into place me, and my little man are on the first thing smokin' and she can do bad by herself.

I make moves to the living room and flip on the TV to check the weather. I need some rain. It's been too nice this past week, and it's fuckin' with my work schedule. Damn, I hate this shit, they gotta do the weather for every other state every time I turn to it. Damn no rain, seems like the hustling god hasn't heard my prayers. I kinda depend on the hustling god to shower my workers with his hypnotic power; there's a science to the rain in the underworld. Now most drug dealers believe the rain brings money because a lot of people stay home, which means there's a high level of boredom which means people need to be mentally stimulated and what can be better than chemical stimuli. All the underworld hustlers love the rain like I do, but I love it not because of boredom power, but for its hypnotic power.

See, my rain theory has a different twist, physiologically the rain rocks my prey to sleep. The rain has a romantic lure and a lot of people make love or get depressed by the gloom. Some people get lazy, some people's bones ache, some people's eyes twitch and best of all the police aren't as alert as they should be. This is when my skill as The Red Silence of Harlem can be best utilized and become as pure and deadly as black rain. Lurking shadows and slouched dark images are no stranger to this hustling god's scene, and as a master in the art of the jux I shine like the darkness of an eclipse.

Two weeks ago I cased out this spot on 139th between Broadway and Riverside. The whole block is infested with Cuban and Dominican cocaine and heroin distributors and my spot is the busiest.

I move to the living room window, expose the pre-rolled Dutch from the side pocket of my shorts and spark it as I flip the scene over in my head and sweat my surveillance skills.

I walked into the building knowing the six men that watched the street from the roof were looking for the pigs, so I ain't sweat them too much. The front door of the building was open and I entered a small area where normally you would press the intercom and be buzzed past the second door. But because the Dominicans run the block and all the tenants are basically hostages in their own homes, the second door's lock has been removed, which is customer friendly.

The lobby hallway is all white and both walls have 12 mail boxes, about 20 feet past the boxes was an open space is. To the left were two apartments and to the right were two more, then directly in front of me was the stairwell. A small security camera hung in the left corner and I assumed it covered only up to the lobby entrance. Over the years, I've either developed or harnessed my peripheral vision to utter perfection so as I passed the second landing, I peeped where the other cameras were without blowin' my spot. The third-floor landing was identical to the second and first, the cameras on the stairwell between the third and fourth floors covered a middle area. But if you make a sharp right, you'll be out of the line of view, then there's not another camera until you reach the front door.

Now this particular floor sells to addicts with daily habits and street generals with big 8th and ounce business. I needed to know how much pedico was kept on hand and how much money as well. I rolled in frontin' like a cokehead with 50 dollars in hand and a concealed magnetized trans-mitter the size of a penny. It's a crazy low-budget bug; I learned how to make it on my last bid, thanks to the manda-

tory trade program. With the help of the New York State correctional system, I became a better criminal.

I walked up to the open door, stepped inside and a dude
with a chrome .357 in his left hand motioned me to move on
to the security guards. The hallway was long and slender; it
was barely big enough for a small linebacker. There were
several doors along the hallway and a large empty living
room at the end of it. I walked to the first door which looked
like it should be a bedroom and two Dominicans were
standing on either side of the entrance, both were holdin'.
One of them pulled out a wand detector and searched me,
then frisked me; good thing I expected this and left my hammer outside in a garbage can. I was allowed to pass and I
proceeded to the large presidential-sized desk with a triple
beam scale on it. A Spanish cat with eyes as big as quarters
was tryin' to hold it down. Money kept lickin' his lips and
scratchin' his nose so it was crazy red; no question the
nigga was ridin' the white horse. That just made my job a
lot easier. With a heavy accent he asked me what I wanted
and I tossed the 50 on the table and pulled out the bug. He
counted the money, then opened the drawer on his left and
scooped out some coke. He started sprinkling it on the scale
and I leaned on the desk like I was thirsty so I could slide
my hand around the edges of the desk and wait for the bug
to snag. And just as planned, my shit did its job.

On my way out, I took a quick count of the window and
rooms and noticed one room with a curtain where the door
should have been. There was a glow of a TV creeping on the
floor. I knew it was the surveillance room. At first, I was a lit-

tle hot 'cause I couldn't see what the cameras could, but later I realized it wasn't a problem. As I left the building, I picked up the heat and a brown paper bag with a Walkman in it. I tossed the aluminum foil of coke on the ground and put the headphones on. I had to search for the frequency that would plug me into pedico central. Amazingly fast I heard my workers as clear as day discussing who knows what. They were speaking Spanish. I hit "record" and FBI'ed the niggas cause later that night I'd take the tapes over to my Spanish momis' house so she could translate. I moved down the block and watched as the customers came and went, and I listened to each other waiting to hear for the jackpot.

I sit on the edge of the bed listening to the tapes and the dark side's sun has risen over its realm. As always my mind races along the tracks of a heist 'cause this is my prayer to the hustling god. I pay homage by never allowing heist moves to leave my mind . . . but—on the real, lately a nigga ain't been true to the power. This dark side done lost its luster, no longer does this game excite me, no more do a nigga jux for fun, no more does the splatter of warm blood entertain me, a nigga done got cautious which calls for closure. I'm a slave to these wicked streets as I was indicted at birth. It was written for me to brandish a gun and dwell amongst these stick-up kids, hit men, hoodrats and four-corner hustlers. For me . . . self-destruction . . . is inevitable.

The recording continues as I listen and search the skies beyond the confinements of these concrete jungles and blood soaked streets. Freedom steps to my weaker half and attempts to creep out and rid itself of this torture I face and a sole tear escapes my ducts. Just then my son enters my peripheral zone, climbs up on my lap and wipes the tear from my face destroying its very existence. Quickly my mind jumps back to my prayers; the hustling god must recognize my worth. I need this one last jux so I can leave this realm with my little man for good.

My son's mother enters the room and I plug the headphones into the stereo. I don't want the hater to know about the new project. When I hit the bonus, there'll only be enough room for two. A few minutes later I pack up the tapes. The night calls to me, it's time to get in the trenches and get this money. My preparation begins with a thick coat of Big's Ready to Die. I put on a jock strap, then the vest. The vest has three 9mm dents in it: one was in the chest when I bought it, the second is in the back panel. One time I pulled a quick unplanned heist in this building on 141st. It went wrong for two reasons: it wasn't raining, and I was acting on impulse.

It was like four summers ago and I just ran up in a number hole so I was a little gassed up, I thought I was the best. I had heard some fiends on the block talkin' 'bout where they were gonna cop from so I followed them. When they walked in the spot I pushed in behind them—face covered and gun exposed. Everyone followed directions and everything went smooth until I tried to leave. I pride myself on my calmness, so instead of running I walked away. Of course the dudes who ran the spot chased me. Now, because the building was in the middle of the block I couldn't take the chance of running to the Ave. and have them blastin' at me-

definite arrest possibility-so I cut through the buildings.

Most of the buildings in Harlem are connected by basement-level alleyways. If you know them right you can go at least two blocks over and up before comin' out; if not you'll still end up a block away. I ran down a small set of stairs thinking I would be able to get away, but a ten-foot razor wire fence fucked that up. I pulled out my blower, hid behind a metal garbage can and waited. Three Cuban niggas came runnin' through the doorway. I started lettin' off shots, two went down, but the third was a lot swifter. He was swift but stupid. After he took cover, he stood up to shoot; he got three to the chest. I breezed out the alley thinkin' shit was clear but as I walked away I got a hot one in the back.

The third hole is in the stomach, I got that one at a party in Wagner Projects. Some kid I robbed remembered my face. But the ill shit is—I didn't even recognize him, I can't remember any of their faces. Sometimes I feel like I know them, but I can't remember where, which is fucked up 'cause I gotta now assume that they were a vic so imagine how much back watchin' I'm doing.

My son likes to watch me get ready for the night; I always let him watch but right now he's gotta bounce. He can't see where the heat is stashed. I expose my partner in crime, insert the clip chamber one in the head and release the safety. The cold steel sends a chill up my arm reminding me of where my thoughts should be, and I finally deal with some shit I been stallin' on. I can't pull this job off by myself . . . I wouldn't have to deal with shit if I didn't fuck myself, but it was necessary. But –

Two weeks ago me and my old partner got these kids from VA. for half a brick and 10,000 big faces. Later we went to the abandoned building where we kept our scale to split the drugs, an M-16 and sometimes money. As we weighed the coke a darkish chill crept through my body. I felt like I was bein' stalked, like a nigga was lookin' to vic me. I brushed it off but the shit jumped up on me again. I stood up and checked the zone for hot triggas but I found nothin'. My man asked me what the deal was, and when I looked in his eyes I saw that sinister cutthroat look. I've seen it many times, and whenever it reveals itself someone ends up with hot lead to the face. I've known him since the third grade and I watched that look go from a general hunger to a deadly cold wolf-like starvation. The stare was always blank like a shark, it's like he's acting on pure animal instinct.

I eased his mind and he turned back to the scale. My heart iced itself cause a nigga had to live by the code, a nigga had to survive, a nigga had to think of his seed first. I know my man was fighting himself because his hunger was beginning to grow, so I did what any real friend would do. I wanted to ease his mind. I didn't want him to have to choose between me and his needs. I quietly removed the hammer from its hiding place and with no hesitation I helped him with his problem and spilled his brains so he wouldn't have to think about killing me. Then I packed up, wiped down and made moves.

I always had a deep darkish love for my man, but I knew he was getting tired of splitting the fruits of our labor. Our

payoffs were getting bigger and bigger, and this one time—
his eyes couldn't hide his hunger pains any more. It was
either him or me, do or die. As he lied there twitching I
wanted to kiss what was left of his face. I wanted to say
goodbye but that was a great sign of weakness so I burned
up the road and left him to the rats. I slid out the back and
made my way through the lot.

Slowly memories of our past invaded my mind. The
nigga was my best friend but his first love was currency. He
was the only nigga whose courage matched my own; no one
could touch our gun game. A lot of niggas be holdin' heat
and quick to pull 'em and quicker to pull the trigga when it's
convenient. But niggas ain't got no heart; pullin' the trigga
before you even aim don't mean shit. How many niggas can
stare down and challenge a nigga's heart when the steel is
in his face? Or how many niggas will test death and grab
the hammer and thug it out for it? How many niggas can be
in a shootout with no fear? How many can look a nigga in
the face and peel his cap back as he cries and begs for his
life? Not enough.

This nigga was one of an elite squad of renegade gun-
slingers, but he was greedy and it was the death of him. His
momz lives in my building and I saw her yesterday. She
asked me about her son and for a hot second I was hurt but
again it's a sign of weakness. So I hit her with my court face
and told her not to worry, he'd show up sooner or later.

There's an art to packing steel, especially in the sum-
mertime. Not only do you have to hide the heat, you have to
move like you don't have it. Unlike a lot of my fellow heat

*holders, I choose not to distort my flow and blow my spot
with a waistband bulge. The jockstrap holds the hammer
nice and snug and allows me to flow freely with no problem.
Suddenly I lose the urge to wear the vest. I peel off the
straps releasing it and put on the all-white tanktop. I slide
on the Ralph Lauren denim overalls and squeeze a black
stockin' cap over the dome and cover it with a fitted aqua
blue baseball hat, just in case niggas wanna start snitchin'.
The oversized 18" Cuban link with frosted Santa Barbara
piece has maneuvered itself around a worthy neck. Next, the
aqua blue and white three quarter Nike Airs with two big
faces and two rug cutters, God forbid I gotta go to the
Island tonight. I stand in front of my full-length mirror mesmerized by the thugged-out Harlem Vibe that shines back at
me and my hata detector goes off. I'm being watched.
Instinct tells me the watcher has negative intentions. My
first reaction is to reach for the hammer, but I'm home so I
know it's my baby's momz. I don't even look at her shysty ass
as I continue to flow. My shine overpowers the crab's mental beef and draws my full attention to it again. There's a
dangerous attraction to my eyes; a courageous nigga with
strong determination and ruthless gunslingin' game is hidden by a lovable heroic killa. And I don't appear to be as
greasy or slimy as one with such horrific thoughts because
of my ability to camouflage it with a smoothness drenched
in malice. Do I appear to be a killer, a jux master, a darkside dweller? Only when it suits me because I am the Red
Silence of Harlem.*

On the way out, I grab two pairs of surgical gloves for

*the no-print jobs, appropriate the cell and finally the jux
tapes. I move to the elevator and my dark-side senses begin
to tingle. It's a hot night and the dark streets are filled. In
this jungle, instincts are the only things that separate predator from prey; even though my identity as the renegade jux
master is a secret, uncooked beef still fills my zone. A lot of
these young niggas be on some "get a rep" shit and my
hand is great so hittin' me for my shine and rockin' it; or
bein' alive after they claim to hit me is all they need to live
off my light. Then there are the cats whose girls wanna be
members of my fan club and can't resist the urge to blow
their cool in my mere presence. Those niggas is the worse
'cause their bullets are hidden by smiles or come from
behind. Faggot nigga be shootin' niggas in the back. It's
worse then Vietnam 'cause I never know where the heat is
coming from. So I decide to merk a U and bounce up to the
roof, surveillance mode. All the roofs on my block are connected so I can creep all the way to the corner, check the
scene and maintain my visual silence.*

*I walk towards the edge, ease down to a full crawl, and
lay across, looking down on all that flows. It's been awhile
since I've watched this dark water flow from the outside. It
seems to be as regular as . . . I wanted to say a sunny day,
but it's been . . . I don't even remember the last time I was
the sun at its peak . . . "The Lion King"! I saw the sun on
that movie. Fucked up right?*

*The streets seem right, I get digital and hit my Spanish
shorty, memory 6. She picks up as always, happy to hear I
made it through another one. I let her know I'll be coming*

through for a translation. Her breathless words trip over themselves as she questions me. I let her know it's all love yet she yearns for conversation in case I don't make it through the night. My thug passion always jacks her heart and she reveals this as she gets stuck verbally like a museum exhibit. She's waiting for the magic words: "I'm coming through

I'll be there in a minute." She gives me the OK and I hang up with a little smile 'cause a nigga's crazy feelin' her. She's the first chic in my life who accepts her position. She's intimidated by the heat, but she knows it's a necessity and she don't stress it. The first time she saw it she said, "Just make sure she don't get in my way."

Myra lives a few blocks away so I make moves on foot. As I stop at the corner the next generation of corner hustlers and gunslingers take time out from their street lessons to practice their pimp game on the local chickens. Whenever they see me they blow their cool, and beg me to put 'em under my wing or just give them the chance to live off my shine. And like many times before, I shut the niggas down, for one niggas ain't worthy to live off my energy and two I can't see myself allowing a —hold up—I feel—a hunger—a hunger like my own. I scan the group of Pepsi generationers and against the wall away from the others is the source of that hunger. Shorty's been watchin' me since I breezed on the block. He hasn't learned to throw shade like a champ yet. I see malice in his eyes, I see the beast waiting to be let out, yeah, —I just found my new runnin' partner. He thinks I can teach him but all I'll be doin' is bringin' out the jux master that's already inside of him. "Yo Shorts, you

holdin'?" He pulls up his sweatshirt and flashes the handle
of a 357, not the best weapon but effective in a robbery. Its
size makes a nigga think twice about resistin' and when you
let off, niggas ain't too quick to be chasin' you. "If I see you
out here tomorrow, I'll know you about money, if I don't . . ."
and I turn and merk off on him. If shorty's real he'll be back
tomorrow; if he's real and hungry he'll be here later tonight
when I come back through the block.

Myra's block is flamin' with Cubans who are looking for
the cat whose been hittin' their workers. Niggas don't even
have a clue who I am, which means can't nobody see my jux
game. The weather got the whole ghetto in the streets tonight
and the energy and action that surrounds me makes me 'noid.
My instinct tells me too much uncooked beef fills these streets
and when it's this much goin' around it's hard to pick up on
the "phd's" and "187s" that are headed in my direction.

The lock of the door to Myra's building was broken back
in the days then I started coming through and I felt a lot
safer if it would lock behind me so I fixed it. My instinct is
on full alert for "ygs" who are novice in this stick-up game
and jux at random hopin' to get lucky and snag a nigga
who's comin' through to cop weight. I use to do the same
thing until I figured out standin' outside and stalkin' niggas
would lead me to thicker pockets. I stand in front of Myra's
door and listen for voices that ain't suppose to be there
—Damn! Myra don't rock like that, fuck's wrong with me,
she's the only chic I met who just loves me for me and not
just for what I can do for her. She doesn't ask me for shit.
She takes care of a nigga, she be teachin' me shit and she's

always tryin' to get me to better myself. She's the one who got a nigga thinkin' he can get out the jungle.

Before I met her, I didn't really understand what it was to receive love. I thought love was . . . on the real, I didn't know what the fuck love was. I useta love my gun, my jewels, gun play, but that shit don't love me back. Myra showed me love. I'm sayin' I know my son loves me but he's a child and somehow he has to love me, but Myra . . . I'm sayin', she ain't gotta go for me living with Tyriq's mother and, why? Does she . . . I guess she sees some shit in me I don't. I think she gives a fuck about me more than I do my muthafuckin' self.

I want to use my key to open the door, but if I do, I'll be robbed of seein' that look on Myra's face when she sees me come in. She always gives me a look of pure pleasure and real love because she's happy I'm still alive.

I'm about to use my usual three-buzz-code, but I decide she'll be more surprised if I ring once that way. . . Shit! . . . not now, I ain't got no time for this shit. My third eye tells me some shit's about to jump off. Slowly I step away from the door using my peripheral vision to scan both sides of the hall. I move to the stairwell, and the strong scent of a cheap imitation Fahrenheit fills my nose—Hispanic male-late twenties and fairly new to the country. The Spanish cats who been here for awhile know better than to come like that. Most likely, hit men brought in, but are they here for me or someone else? Nobody knows I rock here. Fuck it, if I'm wrong some niggas owe me one; they'll probably come looking for me sooner or later, might as well end it now. There's probably two or more, four at the most; two to hold shit down and two for the job that right there tells me these niggas is amateurs. One nigga can take out like ten muthafuckas quietly.

Now the draft that sent the warning signal came from below, the space between the stair banister is like a wind tunnel. What kind of hit man blows his own spot? It's not their fault my skill is crazy on point. I'm like some ole', all five 007 niggas and "Mission Impossible" episodes rolled into one. Muthafuckin' super Harlem nigga. I could take these clowns right here if I wanted to, but that'll bring the heat to my sanctuary. The roof! Watch how easy it is to set these niggas up. I yell "Oh shit." And start running to the roof and they follow. I bust through the door, unleash the hammer, kneel down, and aim chest level. The roof's door opens to the left and from the side of this fixture I'll have a clear shot. I kneel down 'cause instinct causes some of us to turn and look at our height before searching lower. By then—shit'll be blazin'. Their adrenaline rush makes them come through straight amateur style. Stupid niggas thought I wasn't holdin' heat. The first one could of got it right away, but I wanted to get all of them at once, the less shots let off, the less problems. Like I expected, the second one came the same way. All them two niggas heard was the metal slidin', they didn't even get off a shot.

Like I said, I can't have my spot hot: one, 'cause I'm on the run from parole and-two, 'cause police fuck up business for niggas when they're investigating shit, which fucks up my shit too, so it's ghetto graveyard time.

Behind this building is an abandoned one and the lot that's between them is filled with garbage and dead bodies that ain't gonna be found 'til it's time to put up some wel-

fare buildings. I ain't got time to bury niggas so I slip on the surgical gloves and toss both of them off the roof. Before I get rid of them, I flip their pockets, never know what a nig- gas got. A few times, I found niggas who kept their payoffs on them. These two niggas got twin berettas with my favorite 147s-four full clips too. Matter a fact, I'll give one of these joints to youngblood.

Myra greets me at the door with a hug and, "Mmm I missed you Pa. Tu puete come, I made your favorite, arroz con pollo." Then I make myself comfortable and she gives me that disappointed mother look like I broke curfew again. "Pa, you was smokin' wasn't you? What, you stressed out again? Is it Tyriq's punk-ass mother again? The bitch got you in some shit, right? You need to just –no –I'm not gonna fuck with you about her. I understand, Pa, but I just don't like it . . . so don't think I'm mad at you. But . . . on the real . . . fuck that broke bitch. Just cut down on the blunts."

"I'm sayin' boo, a nigga's gotta dull his senses on the dark side."

"There's no dark side when you with me Pa, when you gonna see that? I told you I'm the only one with your best interest in mind. Nobody else gonna do for you like me, and nobody's gonna love you like me. Fuck all the robbin' and stealin' shit 'cause it don't get you nothin' but a bullet in ya ass. I told you, I'll take care of everything until you can get a real job. Just stop with this "Billy the Kid" shit. Please."

"Soon, Ma, soon."

I lounge on the couch and watch Myra make my plate in her sports bra and boxers. Her physique shows how well she can cook, and it's obvious I ain't gonna be able to wear those drawers any more. They seem to have formed perfectly with her wide hips. She walks over to me and the power in each of her steps shakes the floor. Her thighs and calves are crazy brolic and she's unable to walk lightly like she used too, that stairmaster shit ain't nothin' to fuck with.

Her stomach is tighter too, and her tatas are sittin' up on her chest. "Yo you been workin' out?"

"They just opened up a JaQulane on 125th, and me and Nita been goin' every day after work. Why, something's wrong?"

"Na. Hell no. I'm just sayin', yo joints is like logs 'n shit. You walkin' like a monster. I hope you don't wrap those joints around me and crush a nigga's ribs."

"I could never hurt you, Pa," *she says in her I-can-get-what-ever-I-want voice.* "Yo put these tapes on and let me know what's up."

"These from the spot?"

"Yeah the last one, after this—"After this what? *I'm sayin' I know I gotta get out of this living hell but where to, down south? Down south sounds right. I can start all over, put my little man in a good school, get a little electronic 9-to-5 hustle. What about Myra? I can't just leave without her, I don't want to.* "Yo ma you ever thought about leavin' the block?"

"And move where? Like Queens or Yonkers?"

"Na, I'm sayin' leave forever, outta state-type shit."

"With you and the baby?"

"Whatever."

"So wha chu askin' me is do I want to be with you for-

ever?"

"I'm sayin'—"

"Only if you leave your little gun."

"If I get out this jungle, I ain't gonna need it."

I bust down the chicken and Spanish rice like a runaway slave while she translated the tapes. The first tape tells me what I already know: there's five workers, three are security, and one rotates with the distributor in the surveillance room. She begins the second tape, and it seems like I'll be staking the spot out awhile longer until, *"The guy says he wants one and a half. The other one tells Chino to watch him till he gets back."*

"Jackpot stop the tape, that means they keep the weight in the back somewhere. If it was less, he'd keep it in the drawer. Aiight, finish."

"Now he's talkin' to Chino, bullshit though. He wants to know if there's any Spanish clubs around. OK the other guy is back. He says he's gotta weigh the half out . . . take the money Jose . . . count it. He gets mad, he says he doesn't care if he's a regular . . . Chino says he's doin' too much pedico. It's OK, relax it's OK to the customer . . . OK Chino he's leavin'. I'll be back in three days for three and half, Chino says come after eleven, they might be out early because of the nice weather."

"Jackpot, aiight turn it off. The re-up is after eleven which means they'll have more than six bricks. The only thing is gonna be hittin' them before they take the money out. We'll have to hit the pickup man in the building before he gets upstairs without being seen by the cameras." I lean back on

the couch and turn over the scene slowly while thinking out loud. "Where's the blind spot . . . come on I know. . . All I need is a little . . . yeah on the steps going from the second floor. There's a camera on the second looking at the stairs, but there isn't another one until you reach the front door of the spot. Which means they can't see the second set of steps or the area between the steps and the door. So if one nigga comes up behind him on the steps then I can cut him off before he can get to the door. OK, we'll need backup weapons headsets, a getaway car, extra clips, rope in case we can handle it with no bodies, carrying bags, duct tape. We'll have to ride out to Shoalin to sell the weight. Aiight, listen, Myra a couple of days before I rock 'em to sleep I'ma bring my son over. That way we can bounce out the same night."

"What about his mother? What are you gonna—?"

"Fuck her. I'll tell her I'ma take him to visit his grandmother for a week. She'll be happy to get rid of him. I'll call my little brother at Morehouse. He's got a house off campus. We'll stay with him until we can get our own spot."

"Why don't we just—"I know she wants to say let's just leave now but she'll just be talking to the wall.

I roll up some hydro to keep my mind off the jux, I hate dwelling on some shit I already got planned. I start to wonder about the "yg" I saw earlier tonight. I know he'll be there tomorrow when I come through. We'll have to hit a spot before this one so I can see what he's workin' with; if he's not what I want him to be, I'll have to find someone else which will push my shit back too far.

Myra doesn't like for me to smoke, but she understands

why I do, so I watch from the living room as she washes the dishes. Like I said, her thighs are bangin' and it's been a minute since I've been between 'em, a nigga been too busy planning. I clip the Dutch and slide off coming up behind her and resting my hand s on her hips while I inspect her cheeks. I pull her hair to the side and kiss her right behind her ear while sliding my hand up to her chest and release her tatas from that thing she's forced to wear and hates too. She turns and melts in my arms from the power of my thug passion and my hands massage the parts I can't wait to taste. I pick her up as she gasps, knowing she'll soon be getting a nut. I kick open the bedroom, place her on the bed and remove the little bit of clothes she has on. My Mommi doesn't like to be teased so I head right for kitty. I'm the first to do what others have tried. One more reason why she loves the venom from my tongue. It's been awhile and she can't wait. She grabs my head and looks into my eyes and, "I want you inside me Pa."

I enter with no delay as Myra tells me how much she misses me and how she doesn't want me to stop. We flip over as she takes control and I navigate from below, sweat begins to pour down her naked chest and her moaning becomes louder. Her words change to her native tongue, and I know the moment is near. I begin doing my best from below, intensifying the movements until she's frozen by the rush of pleasure fluid and gasps, then, "Aiiiiiii, yo's mios." My job is done.

It's well into Dark side hours when I finally leave Myra's house and again she gives me that look like she's afraid she'll never see me again; that look always gets stuck in my head *like a song I heard before I went to sleep.*

I stand in front of the building, release the Nokia, and dial New Harlem Cab Service, "New Harlem."

"Who dis, Darlene?"

"Yeah, who dis?"

"Red."

"What's the verdict, Daddy?"

"Still swingin'. Yo, 47 workin'."

"Yeah, where you at?"

"152 and Amsterdam."

"Hold on . . . Red, he said he's around your way, give 'em eight minutes."

"Yo Darlene, when you gonna let me shine with you, love?"

"When you can take care of me and my baby so I can quit this slave job and go back to school."

"I hear you love." I've used car 47 for almost two years, and he knows every time I call him, I'm puttin' him on hold for his fee of $35 an hour, hittin' him off with whatever I'm blazin' and a few times we swung an Ep with some chics. Our business relationship has gone way deeper than him just drivin' me around. He's a nigga I talk to about shit that I really should be talkin' to Myra about. Tonight won't be a psyc session; tonight we'll leave the dark side and floss in Harlem's nightlife with the people I once was like.

I stall for a minute so I don't have to stand on the corner too long. This block is flamin' and I'm dirty as hell, so I can't afford to get caught up in a sweep, especially with my heat and its counterpart. At the corner phone, I lounge with the receiver in fake mode to scan the zone for "Phd's" in their many forms and my Uptown chariot that will help me escape these flames. Minutes pass and my chariot appears and again I feel the power I felt earlier in the night. Quickly I search the scene while I breeze to 47 and, there in the same place in the same position, is my new runnin' partner. I open the door, never losing eye contact with him and I feel his malice, his dedication; we exchange ice grills and I pause as my instinct tells me never to submit first 'cause I can never show weakness. I want to smile because his ice face is a defense 'cause he's young, but when he gets older it will be able to take a nigga's heart. To let him know he's worthy to rock in my shine I hit him with a nod and his slow nod answer shows me he doesn't blow his cool and can keep shit quiet.

"What's the verdict?"

"Ain't nothin'," I say as I hand him the heaters over the seat. This chariot is equipped with a steel box under the floor rug next to the brake pedal. Me and many other dwellers stash our hammers and work here. Popo has a habit of pulling cabs over and searching them when they're thirsty to fill their quota. "Anything special tonight?"

"Na."

"I heard Shaka Zulu's got Acapulco gold?"

"Aiight." We ride across 145ᵗʰ brakin' the cultural wall goin' from Spanish on the hill to Black on the way down. Harlem is live at this late hour and my peoples are shinin' so bright that if there was a blackout, the streets would still be glowin'.

We pull up in front of Shaka's and from my position, I

can see the Dru Ham hoes are hard at work doin' their best to flash their assets for the first nigga pushin' somethin' nice. Hoes gotta have a dream, too. Shaka sees me more than my baby's momz and truly I like him better than her. "What's the deal, Shaka?"

"Love, love nigga."

"Let me get a 50 of gold, two 20's of dro, a dime of black and 2 grams of that white girl."

"Damn cuzin', I'm sayin shit can't be that bad that you need that hoe."

"Naa, never that. I got 47 on hold." He looks at me as if he's searching my eyes for the possible fiend in me and hesitates before baggin' up my medication. "Aiight Daddy make sure you stay away from that hoe." I hop back in the tinted window chariot, this time in the front seat, hand my man his poison and strip a Dutch to prepare it for its rebirth. I slam the chunky black and dro into the inner shell of the Dutch, carefully break up the sticky buds, and remove all the pieces which will tear the core while I'm rollin'. Next, I rewrap the outer shell delicately, making sure to keep it tight but not so tight that it disrupts the smooth drags I like to take. The Zippo is exposed, and while I'm lightly drying the Dutch, I notice the perfect shape and form I have recreated, truly one of my best works of art. I almost don't want to smoke it, but that feeling was just that—a feeling— and it will quickly pass. We bounce to the Polo Grounds and stunt for a minute to exchange info, love, and totes when appropriate, then we head for 25th looking for something or someone to get into.

The streets ain't as live as they usually are which means somethin' else has snagged the attention of the nightlifers in my town.

My man, 47, and I lounge in front of the World Famous, heavily indulgin' when I tell my man, "Yo a nigga's cash flow is kinda light, you know, I'm livin' on fumes n' shit. Somethin' gotta come up soon."

"I'm sayin' I know these young niggas who be bubblin' outta town, and all they do is shoot dice and lose money to each other. I took 'em to the Golden Lady last night but they only stayed a minute so niggas is still holdin' somethin'. I'll take you to the block and wait for you around the corner, just float by and act like you wanna get down."

"Yeah, yeah."

We end up on the Eastside, 98th Street, well outside of my territory and 47 pulls into a quiet block. "The buildin' is on the next block. They should all be outside." He reaches into the stash and hands me my hamma' because he knows dice games have a strange way of ending with the winner in a body bag. I cross the Ave and pick up the scent of money which leads to the typical circle of niggas head crackin'. I roll up on the three heads and it's obvious they just came from outta state. Their shines are extra iced their still NY down: Yankees hats, Knicks shorts and jersey, and they're too happy to be home.

"What's the deal, niggas? Can a nigga eat?" The bank holder inspects my wears to make sure I'm able to pay and checks my face for signs of a stick-up kid then,

"Banks 9 and we're shootin' 50 and better, bank rules, no

push on trip 5 and 6. If you push on 6 double bet win or lose."

I hit money with the nod and release my splurgin' money for the weekend. On the next roll I bet a yard off top and bank aced out with a deuce and paid 4 off top. Now there's 5 in the bank and me and the young nigga bet 125 and the kid in the Yankees shirt stopped bank with 250. Bank rolled a 6 and we all pushed and lost; bank now 15. I bet 250 and the rest follow. He aced again, bank back down 750, I spaz out, bet 350 and the other two cats bet 2 and stop bank . . . this nigga hits celo. Now I'm tight as hell I only got 50 left which I'ma risk on a comeback if I get a chance to hold the rocks, so I'm waitin' and waitin' and waitin', banks now down to 5 and the banker ain't been rollin' nothin' over a 5. I bet my last, he rolls a 4. I know I can beat a 4. I'm back in the game. I step into position, shake them hoes until they sound good, and let 'em fall, first roll blank –second roll blank. This time I talk to them hoes shake 'em too long, and . . . tracey.

I step away from my position knowing what must be done. I scan the area for open windows and let my instinct take control. The hamma' appears and, "You know the deal fellas, heaters on the floor first then, the doe."

Niggas was completely asleep. They forgot about the darkside rules. I order them to flip their pockets and make the young one hand me the money. As I back away, I hear him whisper, "He ain't even take the jewels." At first a nigga was tight cause snatchin' a nigga's shine is greasy and slimy; fake thug niggas snatch shines. Shorty ain't know so, "Nigga, this is a job, I ain't got no P.H.D, this shit ain't personal." For the first time, I turn my back on my vics, not because I'm slippin' but because I knew they weren't mad, real. Niggas know fast money goes quicker than it comes and they can take a loss. The vibe these niggas sent was they respected my hustle because they're darkside dwellers too. I also let them keep their shines so they respect my hunger and my life depends on a heist.

The next morning, I wake up with a 'dro hangover and I'm feelin' like I haven't slept long enough. That's that 'dro and gold mixed together. I roll out of bed headed for the bathroom and —yo —it's too quiet. I know I ain't lucky enough to have the house dolo. Na, I can hear my son watchin' "The Lion King." The last time his mother sat and watched a movie with him, she . . . she was in full "hata mode" cause the neighborhood hens told her some bullshit about me and some chic from Espianard. I wonder what new tales from the crypt she done heard about me now. Shit! I really don't wanna hear no shit from her. She always wants to be in some shit with me, fuckin' drama queen. She wants to live a soap opera so bad, dumb bitch. She ain't happy unless somebody said Tad saw so-and-so with blazay, who's supposed to be fuckin' whoever, who used to be married to whoever. And niggas wanna know why I can't live here.

After my bathroom workout, I return to the bedroom to retrieve the half I always leave for the wake up to tranquil-ize myself for the verbal boxing match that's about to go down. I let the effects hit me before I move into the kitchen area which is in the direct line of fire. I'm at the refrigera-tor takin' inventory when. . .

"Yo muthafucka, you just insist on disrepectin' me day in

and day out." I ignore her like always, "Nigga answer me."

"You disrespect yo'self." Damn, I just lit the fuse, after all this muthafuckin' time I ain't learn to shut the fuck up yet.

"Naw, fuck that. I don't disrespect myself. You da one fuckin' every other bitch in Harlem except me."

"We back on that again?"

"Hell yeah, nigga, you ain't got the common decency to put some shade on yo shit."

"Trust me bitch, if I was fuckin mad chics, you damn sure would be the last muthafucka to know."

"What's wrong with my pussy? My shit ain't good enough for you no more? You ain't fuck me in damn near a year."

"So!"

"So! Fuck you Red. You sleep in the same bed with me every night, and you act like I ain't even here." My son turns up the TV, trying to tune us out and, "Why you always yellin' at my daddy?"

"What! Ya little muthafucka, ya should be happy I ain't yellin' at yo ass."

"Yo, don't be talkin to my seed like that."

"What nigga? That little nigga came out my pussy and I'll talk to him the same way I talk to his bum-ass father. Ya broke, bitch-ass nigga. Ya need ta do somethin' with your worthless life —sling rocks, push some weight, somethin'. Do somethin' cause ya little raggedy-ass son is turnin' out just like his punk-ass daddy. The nigga walks like you, talks like you, he even be tryin' to finesse me like you used to —but the shit's weak, just like his no-game-havin', worthless, stupid-ass father. Punk bitch."

Once again I merk off on her 'cause my dark side instincts are takin' over, and I hurt the last person that disrespected my son like that. My jeans and tee shirt is all my temper will allow me to put on along with my shine and hamma and her new counterpart are standard. As I take the money and trees out of the outfit I had on last night, my son comes in the room and a pain fills my chest like straight raw black. I can see the hate develop in his face. His eyebrows never used to arch like that. I almost feel like I'm lookin' in the mirror –the shit's scary. "Daddy, why mommy don't like us?"

"I don't know kicko. Maybe she loves us too much and she don't know how to say it so it makes her mad, and she goes crazy."

"She doesn't love us. When you're not here I hear her talkin' on the phone and she says she wishes you would leave and take me with you."

"Well you know what? She's gonna get what she wants real soon. But that's our secret, aiight? Keep that on the-" and I bend down to his level and I realize I miss my son. He's not as small as he used to be. He doesn't look like a baby anymore, "down low. Everything will be fine in a minute."

I make my way to the spot where my new runnin' partner should be, and the closer I get to the corner, the stronger I feel his presence. Again, there he is in the same outfit he had on the day before, but this time he's alone. For some reason, I can tell he got rid of the rest of his generation to keep his business quiet. I would've done the same thing. I walk past him without sayin' a word, and he follows falling in step at my side. I wish I would've met him at the beginnin' of my stick-up game. We could've taken the dark side by storm. I have plans for shorty for tonight, but his gear ain't gonna fit the scene. We stop on the hill to cop some "fits" and still he's said nothin'.

I grab a button-up Iceberg and fitted to match my kicks and tell shorty, "Get a outfit for the night, kicks too, if you runnin' with me you gotta be camouflaged." I give him a jock strap while he's changing in the dressing room, and he takes it with no question. I pay for everything and on the way out, he asks the clerk where's the garbage. She points to a corner and he tosses his old shit; nigga know this'll be the last time he rocks slum.

We troupe across Convent and I give him a Dutch and the gold to roll while I stop on the low to make a call; I hate walkin' while talkin' on the cell, plus shorty gotta roll that Dutch. Convent is a quiet residential block and the second nicest block in Harlem. There's not too much traffic, and for me, it's one of the safest blocks to walk down when I take a Harlem tour. "What's your name?" He·lights the Dutch, then checks to see if it's burning right and as he blows the smoke out, "Slugga." I smile and laugh silently. I remember the days when I used a name to intimidate people. "Slugga huh. Aiight why?"

"'Cause slugs is my thing."

"Aiight, if a nigga says his name is Quiet Storm what do think that means?"

"Probably 'cause you can't hear the nigga comin' till it's too late."

"Yeah —well that's your new name, and I want you to be

the Slugga who became a Quiet Storm."

"I feel you. So what do I call you 'cause everyone calls you somethin' different?"

"Figure out a way to call me without callin' me. Let's take it to the next level of ebonics. The crackers done labeled it so its power is bein' drained. Let's always be two steps ahead of the game. niggas can't stop what they can't catch up too."

We stop at a hydro spot and cop three more 20's, then the bodega for two cases of Corona before making our way to 130ᵗʰ and Convent. I only trust three women in the world: Myra and the dooby sisters, Kenya and Nonye—two women who are true troopers; they're dedicated to gettin' money with a nigga if they see his worth. They know how to mold a nigga who hasn't recognized his worth yet and then make him shine as his hand calls for. They're like hustling teachers who do their job because they love Harlem, not because they're grimy money hoes.

As we enter the building, I wanna test Storm's instinct so as we approach the elevator, I let him walk ahead of me. Now the building has a lot of blind spots and a nigga could be a victim with ease. By peepin' Storm's skill in this stick-up labyrinth, a nigga can tell what he's workin' with. The elevator is directly across from a stairwell, and as I press the button, Storm looks through the staircase window to check it. If we would've just hopped on the elevator, a nigga could've ran up behind us and stuck us in the elevator. He gets 20 points for that. On the 19ᵗʰ floor, he steps out first –nigga definitely got heart. He doesn't even know what he steppin' into. It's kinda stupid though. You always gotta check the scene first, but he's young. When he gets to my level, he'll learn to let the heat come to him. This way it has to come on your territory, and you'll have the advantage. The calmer you are, the easier it is to peep out a scene whatever it may be. I motion to the left with a nod and we step off together, floating down the hallway like two smooth criminals on our way to take over the world. Again, I motion with a head nod to the next apartment, and before I can lift my hand to reach for the bell, he puts his ear to door –quickly, "What chu listenin' for?"

"I'm sayin', you ain't sayin' where we was goin' so I figured it's some chics and I know the Coronas ain't for no niggas. So if I heard some nigga's voices, I'd ask you if they're suppose to be there, if not then –"He scored a quick 50 with that one. I didn't expect him to read the situation like that, matter fact he gets another 20 for surprising me.

"I'm sayin' I don't trust nobody but I trust both of these chics like I trust my heat with a full clip." I ring the bell with my code, "Always have a bell code with someone you trust, if you don't buzz the same, they know shit ain't right."

There's a moment of silence on the other side of the door then, "I don't even have to see who it is 'cause I know that ring and the nigga on the other side's got beef 'cause we ain't seen you in a minute."

Kenya opens the door and we follow her to the end of the hallway to the living room and she sits on the loveseat in ankle socks, a cut- off fitted DKNY, and spandex.

"My nigga, The Red Silence of Harlem, I was wonderin' when you was gonna come through."

"What you thought, I was dead or somethin'?"

"Never that love, I know niggas can't kill what they can't

see."

"*True, true. Where's Nonye?*"

"*In her room. Who's this?*"

"*This is my new partner Storm, Quiet Storm.*"

"*He's got the same look you had back in days, Red, but he's got a teacher so he won't make the same mistakes.*"

"*Storm, leave a case here and put the rest in the freezer.*"

The nigga walks in the kitchen inspecting the apartment well, with now shade, and Kenya smiles and winks at me. Yeah –she sees somethin' in him she likes which means I made the right choice. Nonye creeps into the room. She walks as light as a cat—no sound. Shit used to drive me crazy because she's the only person who can sneak up on me. Nonye flashes her famous, mind-melting smile which puts any nigga in range under her spell, usually her and Kenya'd be rockin' the tightest doobies ever to come through Harlem, but the heat's got'em pinned up.

Many women who lived on the dark side as long as they have show signs of breakdown; see this darkside shit is like a soul sucking' hell. The shit drains the life right out a muthafucka, but somehow Kenya and Nonye managed to stay petite and unblemished over the years. I've known them almost ten years and a nigga went from peach fuzz to a goatee, from reckless to relentless, from crazy to calculated, and still they look as good as they did the day we met.

"*Yo, Kenya, tell my man how we met.*" *He's gotta feel like part of the family so he won't cut his own throat –if he fucks up with me, I gotta lay his shit to rest. Tonight he's gonna learn a lot and this'll be the beginnin' of a life with*

the dooby sisters. They don't know he's gonna be takin' my
place in their life. I should tell 'em I'm getting out—they are
my peoples—not yet – I'll tell 'em when I'm on my way.

"Me and Nonye were in this club called M.K's –back in
the days it used to be a ballin' spot. So we in there havin'
drinks, and I see Red and immediately I knew he didn't
belong there. It wasn't something every one else could
notice. He had a fresh cut and a nice outfit on but he ain't
had no jewelry and he wasn't havin' a good time. Every
nigga that's getting it wears jewels of some kind and even if
they're not really havin' fun, they act like they are. Now I
can tell he's a young nigga and he's camouflaged so I watch
'em to see who he's watchin'. Again, I can tell he's young
'cause he's watchin' the nigga a little too hard. Now I'm
thinkin' heist or hit, but his face ain't hard enough to be a
hitman. What he didn't know was the guy he was watchin'
had two bodyguards that never played him close and only
followed him like the feds. I could tell Red was better than
average, but he didn't have the right teachers. So I walked
over to him, put my hand where I knew the gun would be,
and what did I say Red?"

"If you were as silent as good as his body guards, you
could've got him a long time ago; that's where The Red
Silence of Harlem was born."

"And I walked back to my table. Then after about a half-
hour, he comes over –me and Nonye done already discussed
how long it would take him. Then he sits down and doesn't
say anything; he always knew when to speak and when to
stay quiet. Finally Nonye says, 'roll with us for a minute

*and you'll be so good, niggas won't mind being hit by you',
and it was on ever since that day."*

*Kenya and Nonye don't smoke but they like to get con-
tact; they say cigarettes and blunts make their lips dark,
somethin' they can't have. They sip on the Coronas and I
have moved next to Kenya on the loveseat. Oh yeah, me and
Kenya been sex friends for years now —Storm has already
fallen victim to the smooth chocolate legs that Nonye has
extended across his lap on the couch. I pull out the beretta
I got from the clown-ass hit man in Myra's buildin' and pass
it to Storm and, "Get rid of that cannon." His eyes light up
as he tries to hide his emotions. "Aiight listen close, that's
a .45 beretta with a built-in silencer which only works with
subsonic bullets they won't break the sound barrier and
make noise. The grain is 147, the best on impact. They rip
right through the body, killin' instantly. If a nigga happens
to live, it won't be long enough for him to talk. You don't
want those joints that stay in a body 'cause niggas survive
with those." His eyes are chinky from the trees, but I can see
him absorbing the information.*

*"If a nigga manages to get away and runs on a flat, get
down on one knee, grab it with both hands, look down the
barrel, and aim for his back—the farther he is, the bigger
the hole in his chest'll be. Next, never get too attached to
someone or somethin' that you can't walk away from in a
heartbeat. 2 —emotions are a weakness. Never jux for
revenge or outta anger and jealousy. 3 —don't do a jux if
your heart ain't in it. If you ain't feelin' it, let it ride. 4
—never get too close to a vic, you might get a nigga who'll*

grab the heat and take it. 5 –greed and hatred can distort the relationship to the work. 6 – move effortlessly. And finally the only time we hit spots is in the rain or after it rains. As time goes on, you'll understand why."

"But we catch a vic whenever?"

"Whenever, wherever, if it feels right. Any other questions?" He shakes his head "no" as he inspects his new extension of his body and Nonye says, "I like him—he don't ask no questions—that means he'll follow orders and stay quiet." I've seen that look in Nonye's eyes before but it was comin' from Kenya the moment she seduced me. Once I heard them talkin' about me while I was in the bathroom and Non asked Kenya why she turned me out and she said, 'Niggas trust you better when they know you'll be there in the morning. And niggas only worry about two things: money and sex; if you take the sex off their mind, they focus on getting paid."

Kenya knows I've done my part for now and I've been strokin' her thigh for the past 20 minutes so she decides to lure me into her room so Nonye can begin part two of Storm's training and so we can renew an old friendship. "Red, I wanna talk to you alone for a minute," she says, givin' me a steamy, yet warning look. If I resist in any way, I know I'll regret it so I follow her without a thought. Nonye and Storm speak briefly before she says, "I have somethin' I wanna give you." Then she gets up and floats to the entrance heading to the back rooms and looks at Storm, who is momentarily stuck in his seat by the gold. She gives her famous smile which lifts him to his feet and sends him helplessly following. She walks passes Kenya's room, knocking twice, giving whatever signal the knock means before bringing Storm into her web. "Storm, if you gonna be workin' with Red you'll need somethin' to help calm your nerves when you get stressed and agy, you know when things get too hectic. Sometimes smokin' weed ain't enough so every time you have that problem—"

She pulls up her tee shirt and the room is fairly lit by the dark side's sun so he has no problem admiring the shapely form of her body. She pulls off her panties and prowls to him and hands him her gift, "Take these out your pocket and put them up to your nose and when you smell them you'll remember everything we've done together." She removes the beretta from his hiding place, sending a chill up his spin. She tosses her tee shirt to the side, allowing him to praise her every curve as she guides his hands over her body. She undresses him, then leads him to her classroom. He kisses and licks and she's happy he's somewhat talented. Then she decides to test how well he follows orders. She invites him to meet the places he will never be able to forget and he accepts. At first, she directs the venom of his tongue but it wasn't long before he was able to find his place under the sun. Storm is patient and persistent and truly isn't selfish when it comes to pleasing. She moves to step 3 where the real test would come—is the Quiet Storm able to ride to the last stop? She led in the beginning, believing he would get caught up in the waves of her sea, but she soon lost control and Storm put her back on track, and she's happy he's in the advance class before his time.

Nonye loves being in her purest form while she stands in

the window and lets the breeze caress her body. Storm remembers his mentor telling him emotions are a weakness, but he can't resist the feeling he gets as Nonye's physique reflexes the rays of the dark side's sun. He's never understood what beauty meant until just at the moment when he could find no other words to describe the vision that is before him. She walks to the dresser, still bein' watched by her new student and opens a jewelry box. She removes a 22-inch Cuban link and puts it around her neck without opening the clasp. She floats back to the bed with the chain's links resting between her naked breast and, "I like to put chains in my mouth when they're dangling on my chest." She removes the chain and slips it around Storm's neck, "When you do your first job, I want you to buy a piece for it so you'll be properly camouflaged. Niggas won't ever see you comin' Quiet—" and she kisses his chest, "Storm." And kisses his chest again and class is in session once more.

DAY BREAK

Von

My vision clears as I wake and see the face of the woman I love more than life itself. I watch her still asleep as I have done many times before, admiring her pure wholesome beauty, the beauty that has captivated me since the day we met. Her eyes are hazelnut shaped and deep chocolate brown with lashes that extend perfectly. Whenever I speak to her, I can see she's listening to me. A lot of times people have an almost blank stare on their face and you know they're just waiting their turn to speak. But not Ebony, it's like she searches my soul for the words that exists, between the words; its like she's feeling everything, not just listening.

Her mouth is almond-shaped and her lips are like full cushions of luscious comfort; many days I have enjoyed their light gentle pressure when placed on my neck. Her skin is like the smooth calmness of a silent ocean. She has become a piece of my life that I can't imagine being without; she is the love that completes my life. We've been together every weekend for the past thirteen months and now, more than ever, I'm thinking about makin' it permanent.

When we first met, I was on some real bullshit, and Ebony didn't even kiss me 'til like our third date. I wasn't used to that, but I tolerated it 'cause I saw somethin' special. I'm glad I did though 'cause right about now, I'm the luckiest man alive. Eb has helped me keep my head straight and focused on my goals and she says I'm the first man she's been with who can take her breath away with a kiss, a smile or a touch.

The room is completely dark, except for the sun, which is able to creep through the cracks of the venetian blinds and navy blue curtains. I can't have the sun waking me up at the crack of dawn. Being woken unnecessarily is something I can't have. Eb says the room is like being in a cave. My work schedule usually calls for me to be up two days at a time and sleep has become a rare commodity. I ease out of bed trying not to disturb Ebony's sleep, because our evening of lovemaking was more of a TaeBo workout. I approach the dresser to retrieve the necessary after-shower attire and open the sock drawer. The first thing I used to see was an assortment of Tim' and Nike socks and various patterned boxers. Now I gotta search through Ebony's Victoria's Secret treasures to get what I need. First, the golden teddy, then purple, the violet, the black and teal are now intertwined with Timberland, and there's so many bra and panty sets in here I can't even see my boxers. I dig through her feminine pleasurables and find what I need.

I look around my dim room and notice how she subtle-ly taken over; it's like her stuff just started accumulating. She's made space for her shoe collection in the corner where my weights used to be. The brown-cushioned chair which is used for the "not dirty yet" pile of clothes is full with not only my jeans but hers as well. My dresser is cleaned and organized. My closet has been invaded by skirts, blouses and dresses, and my sneakers and boot boxes are crowded by the other half of her shoe collection. I'm not exactly sure how the shit happened, but in the last year, she's managed to merge with my bedroom. She's claimed her territory, and I didn't have any wins in her conquest for the planet of a Vikin' nigga. No question I used to live in straight Vikin' mode, but, Ebony started coming around and shit changed. Not only does she regulate the cleaning situation, but she's also made some room for all the things I bought her in our three-year relationship. The petals from the first dozen white roses I bought on her birthday are in a jar on the dresser along with a black-mink teddy bear from the day she left for school. That was a long year for us. Because I was workin', I couldn't visit her up at Boston College as much as we wanted, and even though we did see each other whenever we could, it still wasn't enough.

I walk across the hallway to the bathroom, and once again I'm reminded of Ebony's invasion. At one time, the sink only had a tube of toothpaste on it, and the medicine cabinet was empty except for mouthwash, aspirin, alcohol, and bandages. Now there's body gels by the toothpaste, and facial scrubs, masks, and creams are crowding my alcohol. Bath jells and puffy things on ropes are in the shower. The cabinet, where only towels and Q-tips dwell, has been attacked by four different types of shampoo and conditioners. Curling irons of all sizes, combs, brushes, some kind of stone for her feet, nail polish, perfume, tampons, vaginal cleaner, and to top it all off, the aroma of Pinesol has been replaced with –potpourri. Once my mother told me that love would take over my life when I wasn't lookin' and sure enough, she spoke the truth.

I come out the shower and put on my official New York Knicks shorts and ankle socks on and retire to the kitchen. It's my turn to make breakfast. The hallway walls leading away from the front door, bedroom, and bathroom are covered with the accomplishments of my short musical production career. Plaques of three gold records and other framed albums I worked on hang side-by-side with three blown-up pictures of me and Ebony. One is of us at her grandmother's birthday party in Maryland; her uncle June-June likes to get those natural setting shots. In this one, he caught us leaning across a lawn table talkin'. I don't remember what we were sayin' but the two of us are lookin' deep into each other's eyes and she was smiling with her hands on my face. From that picture, you can really see how much we love each other. The other two are from Thanksgiving at my mother's house in L.I.; in one, she's feeding me something and she insists on babying me. In the other one, we're cheek-to-cheek with the ill cheese grin.

The livin' room of my cozy one-bedroom apartment is

basic. The black-felt couch is against the wall to the right with wooden end-tables on both sides. Adjacent to that is the matching loveseat. All are focused around the entertainment center. The Magnavox 32-inch TV sits on a wooden stand with wheels; under that is the VCR equipped with cable box compatibility, four speed slow motion, high-speed rewind and auto tracking. On the cart on the right is a receiver tape deck and CD player which is hooked up to the VCR and connected to four Kenwood speakers. Below, the sound equipment is the Playstation game system and an assortment of cartridges. To the left of the TV is a 100-space CD rack with everything from Bobby Womack to the Infamous Mobb Deep. Then on a rack in the corner between the stereo and speaker is my most prized possession: every karate flick made by the Shaw Brothers and Ocean Pacific. There's *"The Crippled Avengers"*, *"36 Chambers,"* *"Shoalin vs. Lama,"* *"Fist of The White lotus,"* *"5 Elements,"* *"Mystery of Chess Boxing,"* *"8 Diagram Pole Fighter,"* *"Hells Wind Staff"* and so many more. At last count there were 85, and that was six months ago.

When Ebony and I first met, she couldn't deal with my obsession with karate flicks until I showed her a few with women martial artists who were better than most of the men. Later, when we watched them, I broke everything down so she could understand why they always spent a large part of their lives trainin' to avenge their brother's death. She eventually became as open as I am. It was important Eb enjoy watchin' them as much as I do because they're a part of my world, and I wanted her to be a part of the things I love to do.

The aroma of my world-famous cheese and onion omelet will soon fill the apartment. When I was young, my mother worked nights and many meals were cooked by Big Von a.k.a. D-licious. Living alone forced me to hide my culinary skill, so the many women I talked into cookin' for me would remain in the dark. One night, Eb popped up unexpectedly and caught me making lemon chicken with rice and garlic potatoes. I tried to make excuses so I wouldn't have to cook for her, but she wasn't havin' it. On my birthday, she bought me a set of stainless steel cuisine pots—one of those gifts that are really for the giver and not the givee.

As I mix the ingredients for the omelet, I hear the shower running and slowly my mind blurs like the pieces of this puzzle that will create a masterpiece. Last summer, I switched to clear shower curtains and it took Eb awhile to get comfortable enough to shower with the door open. The closer we became the more she never wanted to end a conversation just to get in the shower.

One night, all the lights went out in the building, one of Con Ed's famous late-night accidents. Eb was in the shower and as I walked to the bedroom, I got a glimpse of her. The window above the shower allowed the moonlight to reflect off of her wet body, causing her skin to glisten like a calm ocean at night. Her hair was up in a bun, and I couldn't see the exact features of her goddess-like shapely body, only its silhouette. I watched her only because I could do nothing less. I don't remember how long I stood there, but every time I hear the shower running I think about that day.

I set two places on the table and decorate Ebony's plate with parsley. Once, when we were out at dinner, she mentioned how cute she thought parsley was, and right about now, I'm in a make-her-smile mood. The past few months I've been more concerned with her happiness then my own. I'm sayin', I always wanted her to be happy, but now it seems like her happiness and well-being are the most important thing in my life. Every time I'm at work, I get these visions of doing something with her to make her feel wanted and needed.

I return to the stove to make sure the omelet doesn't stick to the pan and hear Ebony's bare feet entering the kitchen. She wraps her arms around me sendin', a message which thanks me for the pleasure I've brought to her life. She puts her hands on my chest, places her face on my shoulder blades, and lets out a soft moan, as if she's been relieved of a heavy mental burden. I flexed a little somethin' 'cause a nigga can't resist the urge, and as she pulls away, she kisses my shoulder and, "I thought it was my turn to make breakfast." Then she walks to the table with nothin' on but a towel. She folds her left leg under her as she sits, totally revealin' her petite curvaceous yet somewhat voluptuous thighs which I've laced many times with the soft touch of my lips. Ebony always likes to walk around in a towel or one of my T-shirts or tank-tops after a shower. She very rarely, almost never wears panties in the house; she says they restrict her and as she would say, "I need my essence to breathe." When I heard that, I decided to replace my extra-large bath towels which cover her to her knees with smaller ones which come just below her perfectly shaped, cute butt, and I can't resist the chance to see her thighs.

"I'm sayin', I already made my world-famous omelet so you can just cook the next two times."

"To tell the truth—I knew if I stayed in the bed long enough, you'd get up and— … Is that parsley?" she whispers and a warm tingle creeps up my spine. I love to see that surprised look on her face. She rubs her hand down my leg as I stand over the table, and she fills the room with an almost heavenly glow of a smile and, "You know I don't like surprises." I know she doesn't but I couldn't help it, I love her. "So what's on for the day, Von?"

"I gotta get the Ac washed and I'ma pick up my shine from Ted. I had him put some chips in the pendant and polish the chain. And my aunt Alicia said there's a sale at the Yonkers Mall, so after I go to the bank I'm gonna." My mother told me I had to start thinking 'bout me and Ebony as "us" or we'll always be "him and her", then end up just "him." Eb used to beef about that too but now she notices my attempt to include her in my life and lately she ain't been commentin' about it as much. "We can go shoppin'." She acts as if she didn't hear me correct myself and, "And you're goin' to the barbershop, right?" she says with a hint of sarcasm.

"Oh yeah?"

"I'm sayin', you're still handsome, hairy or not, but! That perfectly shaped curly fro and goatee I fell in love with is looking scraggly. I've got a 10:30 appointment to get a touch-up so you can drop me off on your way to get the car washed and pick me up after you leave the shop. OK sexy."

And she wipes food off of my mouth and, "No doubt, it's your world for a minute."

"How about it be our world for a minute." she says as she laces me with a full-lipped kiss, "No question."

It's 8:30 and I'll only take my usual 20 minutes to get dressed but as always Eb'll be ready in an hour or two so ain't no leavin' early. If I try to get dressed now, I'll just be in her way which will make her take longer, so I charge up the Playstation and try to complete my season on NBA Live 2001. Then I grab the remote and fill the crib with the sounds of The Ticalian Stallion and Mr. Funk Doctor Spock; on the low, this seems like a new way of life for me. Ebony buzzin' around the crib getting dressed and me waiting on some real "couple" shit. I'm kind of diggin' it. See, like a lot of my people, my pops was a crab, around but not around so being in a complete family scene is something I've always wanted. And right about now, I got a feeling I'm gonna be happy for a long time. The ideal of me DaVon Josia Davis, a.k.a. Big Von in love at 26 thinkin' 'bout movin' Ebony in and plannin' a future is some real next shit. For a minute, I was truly living the single life to the fullest.

In 1991, I was in my second semester at B.M.C.C. and strugglin' to hold on to my career as a dancer. Gangster rap had exploded on the scene and took the industry by storm, making' video dancers obsolete. Gone were the days of hip-house and club joints like "The Chubster" and "I'm Caught Up" at 112-115 beats per minute. Everything quickly changed to hard scary beats that no one could dance to. I was forced to resort to teachin' a dance class to pay the bills; it was lucrative but not fulfilling, and I ended up hanging out with most of the groups I used to dance for. All I did was blaze trees and watch cats create the demonic bullet-ridden sounds that destroyed my career. I was there so much I learned to do what they did and just as good as them. Soul Style Sound Studio was my first job.

After only six months of being in the right place at the right time with the right sound, I went from late-night engineer to lead engineer which paid a little $17 an hour on-duty and or $3,000 a session off-duty plus studio fees.

A year later on my 21st birthday, I moved out of my momz house and into my own one-bedroom on 130th and Convent, Harlem USA baby. For the first year, all I did was have house parties and all-night smoke sessions with my squad, and with a new crib came a harem of woman at my disposal. I was spendin' money like the Sultan of Iran. Yo, I was straight-up money whylin', dice games, trips to nowhere, and Moet flowin', I was buggin'. Funny how God comes through and changes your life when you least expect it.

Ebony is in the final stages of her primping ritual. I know cause she breezes by in shoes, stockings, a skirt and bra, and gives me a look like "why am I not getting dressed." Of course my dressing escapade is nowhere nearly as complex and calculated as hers, but being from Harlem, you know it's a science to how my shit is done. My Calvin Klein jeans are already waiting for me on the no- dirty-yet chair, I grab a white Fruit of The Loom tank top and T-shirt, slide on the all-white Nike Airs, pull out the CK jean jacket and navy blue NY Yankees hat, and I'm ready to go.

Simple, yet I'm in official superstar mode. While I'm clos-
ing the clasp on my Figaro bracelet, Ebony looks at me
slightly disgusted because in the three years we've been
together, she's never seen me take any longer then a half-
an-hour to get dressed. Once I bet her she couldn't get
ready before I did and she didn't even come close. For two
weeks, she had to be my maid, and I did everything possible to make it extra hard for her. She's been trying to get
back at me for that for the last three months.

I stand at the door still waiting when a vision hits me:
it's our wedding day and I'm standing at the altar looking at
my watch and sweatin' 'cause she's like four hours late. "I
hope you don't take this long on our wedding day." Quickly
she pokes her head out of the bedroom like a scared deer,
"Our wedding day? We're getting married?" Damn! Why'd
I say that? Now she's gonna wanna have a week-long discussion about it. Once, I said I wondered what our kids
would look like—I ended up enduring a four-day discussion
on how she needed to finish school first. I just wondered, I
wasn't proposing we have kids right away, just what if and
what would they look like, but as usual, she went off the
deep end. Now with new shit, she'll be expectin' a proposal and wantin' to go ring shopping. Or she'll be going on
and on about why we shouldn't get married so soon. So, to
prevent the headache, "No. I said every day. I hope you
won't continue to take this long every day."

"Oh I was wondering what that was all about."

Last night I managed to get a parking space right in
front of the building; if you live in any large populated city

then you know how valuable a good parking space is. After a long hard day at work, it might be worth killing someone for. And on this beautiful sunny day, my 1999 two-door Acura coupe with chrome-dipped five stars is looking as good as it did the day I drove it off the lot. I saved a whole year to get the Ac, I cut back on everything; I practically lived off of soup and sandwiches. I didn't go out; I used candles at night; I even got rid of my cable box. I felt like that was the roughest twelve months of my life. Originally, I wanted to get it in money green but I ended up settling for a metallic burgundy with beige leather interior, power sun/moon roof, 12 disc CD changer, and power everything. As fate would have it, burgundy is Ebony's favorite color; I guess that's what got her attention the day we met.

We met the day after my birthday. I was a co-host at Club 21; my man Ted's b-day is after mine so we had a party together. I was in front of the club in full sultan mode while Ron G filled the streets with his hot mixes by way of my Sony speakers. I was with two of my peoples when Ebony and her female crew flowed on the scene. They thought it was a regular night and when the bouncer told them it was a private party and entry was by invite only, one of them proceeded to lay her game down to get them in. Because I was shinin', Ebony could do nothin' less than notice me. Then she blessed me with eye contact and with the swiftness I hit her with infamous lip-lickin' eye wink. Next thing I know it's three years later, and I'm spending almost every day with her.

The Ac has a dust coat on it which is causing an extremely dull shine, and it kind of hurts me to see it look so bad; I'ma take care of that right away. Before I pull off, I crack the sunroof and bless the CD with the sultry sounds of Sade. Eb didn't like Sade when we first met, but after we made love to my all-time favorite album "Promise" a few times, she came to see Sade in a new light.

In my neighborhood we are known as "that cute young couple" from the 400 building, and all of the older-timers like to see us together. They're constantly giving their blessing and advice on how to have a successful relationship. Whenever I see any of them, I make sure I stop and talk for a minute. I don't mind, you know: I figure I can learn from their wisdom and not end up alone and unhappy. I was raised to always listen to what my elders have to say; young people listening to them seems to make them feel good, and I can't deprive them of this feeling. I guess they like to be reminded they're still needed by someone. I see a lot of them alone and very rarely do any of their families visit them. They all treat us like one of their children, so I treat them like one of my grandparents.

As I approach Manhattan Ave, "Hey Ms. Jenkins." I pull over to a three-story brownstone, hop out, and make moves to the elderly and still beautiful Ms. Jenkins. She's 80 but she looks about 50, some 'ole real Lena Horne ageless beauty treatment. "How you doin' today Ms. Jenkins?"

"Just fine. Where's that wife of yours?"

"That's her in the car."

"Oh —you know I can't see a damn thing without my glasses. Well, you just tell her I said hello."

"You need anything from the store?"

"No, I'm fine. Now go on and take care of that wife of yours and don't forget to tell her you love her every now and then. And don't listen to those boys who don't have no girl-friends. And listen to her when she talks 'bout what you don't do, alright?"

"Yes."

"Go on now."

"Talk to you later."

"Mm hmm." Same thing every time. She stays hittin' me. She's been living in Harlem more than 55 years, and I've learned more from her about black history and music than any class could ever teach me.

We near one of the many tenement buildings Uptown, and I honk the horn and throw the hand up for the "what up" to the four men playing cards on a fold-out table. Usually, I'm allowed to get away with just an acknowledg-ment but it's been a while since they've hit nigga in the head so, one says, "Hey youngblood, come on over and holla at us a minute." Ebony rolls her eyes as I get out to converse with these retired playas that once terrorized the women of New York with their slick hypnotic venom and smooth mind-melting flows and now they spend their days playing cards and passing jew-els to the next generation of playas who have excepted the royal scrolls of venomism.

"What's the word, cat daddy?" the one called Nunu says.

"Everything's everything."

"That's the little woman in the ride?" says Ice.

"Yeah, no question. No one else can hold that spot down like her."

"Now ya see, this youngblood is a true playa. Not only does the boy stay sharp, he keeps a sharp woman with him and the nigga knows how to treat her!" says Ice.

"Let me hit you in the head one time. Give that young girl everything she needs and make her proud to say she's your woman. That way you won't end up hangin' out with your boys for the rest of your life like us." says Nunu.

"I hear you." I give them all love and head back to the ride, never brushing off the remarks they make. I get in smiling, and Ebony asks, "What'd they say, *now?*"

"They told me keep you smilin' and give you whatever you want and need."

"See, I always said you should listen to them."

"Yeah, right." At one time, Eb didn't understand why I always stopped and talked to the o.t.s. in the neighborhood; she grew up in Maryland and moved to New York when she was 14.

In Maryland, the majority of people have lived around each other all their lives and they know each other's families, which makes interaction inevitable. In New York, people live next to each other and may never speak, and people move in and out and a lot of people are only in one place three to five years at a time which means any bonds created are treasured.

I've only lived Uptown for 5 years, and because I respect and have a deep love for Black people, I find it hard not to pay homage to the ones who help me to be what I am. In New York, a cold heart is a necessity and someone coming from another state to live has to develop one in order to survive amongst it. Ebony just developed one, which makes her withdrawn from people she doesn't really know. I, on the other hand, see these Harlemites as my extended family because I, like them, am the heart of Harlem. Even though we weren't born and raised here, we are Harlem; we are official Harlemites; we are a family.

It's 10:15 and 25th, which is the center of Harlem, is beginning to come alive. The stores prepare for people of all ages and low income to spend their hard-earned scraps on false power that comes along with pretty shiny things they have to offer. I stop at the corner of 125th and Lenox and across the street I see a line of about 25 people waiting for the check-cashing place to open. That many people waiting at this time of day must mean it's either the 1st or the 15th, the days when all welfare recipients pick up their scraps from the government, and when every drug dealer in NY has a smile on their faces. At one time, I felt sorry for the multitude of people forced into this situation, but the older I got the more I grew to hate them. These are the same people who were supposed to feed my generation's minds and help us to grow and walk on the straight and narrow path. They were supposed to teach us how to become adults, but instead they allowed TV to raise us. They allowed crack to steal our role models and left us to care for ourselves which meant the streets fed our minds. Now they call the police on their children and let them shoot us in the back. They let the government put guns in our babies, hands, and the media tells them their own children are uncontrollable. They let us drop out of school to make hundreds of thousands of dollars a day stripping in some club or to make porno movies, or sell plastic viles with red, pink, and blue caps. They let us have a false belief we can have anything we want if we have enough money. They allow us to think we won't become one of they many statistics of the criminal justice system. And as we sell death in a bottle, sell our bodies, and shoot ourselves, we watch as the ones who were supposed to protect and teach us, support the twisted shit they put us in. Yo, how you gonna watch a girl who could be your daughter, sister, or cousin take off her clothes?

I drop off Ebony at *Beauty Now*, not forgetting to kiss her goodbye; once, when I did, she had a fit, said I didn't love her. Later, I realized it was all an act to get me to never forget to kiss her again. I cruise across Lenox Ave now listening to the offbeat martial arts music and lyrics of the Wu. I hope Ebony'll be ready by the time I leave --Damn. I pick up my cell and dial the number to Levels Barbershop, whose motto is being a star is only a state of mind.

"Superstars."

"Yeah, this Von, Kazo there?" The voice at the other end says, "Yeah, hold on. Yo Ka, phone." There's a pause and I hear the receiver banging against the wall as it dangles.

"Yo, dis Kay."

"Yo, it's Von. What's the word?"

"Ain't nothin', you comin' in today?"

"Yeah, I'm on my way to get the ride clean. Hold me down around 10:30."

"Aiight, if you ain't here by 10:45, you gotta go after the

next head. Yo, you still on for the picnic, too?"

"No question, you ain't even gotta ask."

Kazo's been my barber for the last five years and as a part of the Levels family, I've got the advantage of making an appointment so I don't have to wait in line. Most shops you have to wait, which can be an all day project if you don't get there early enough, but at Levels appointments help to keep the day flowing.

I cross the 145th street bridge which connects the Boogie Down to Harlem; my favorite car wash is on the Bronx side. The cats around my way who're pushin' somethin' nice pay dudes 15 to 20 dollars to get that personal touch. I, on the other hand, pay 5 and give the Ac my own touch; nobody's gonna take care of mine like me. I drive up to the entrance and my man Antar hits me with the smile. "What up Ant?"

"I'm doing well and you?"

"I'm good. How's your kids?"

"They're all fine."

"Aiight. Yo, did you check out that security job I told you about?"

"Yes, the lady told me to come next week and take a test."

"See I told you. And the money is better than here."

"The only bad thing is I won't see you anymore."

"Yo, if you get that job I'll be happy I won't see you." Antar is from Tanzania. He says out of all the people that come through, I'm the only one who kicks it with him.

After a quick wash, I pull out the tools for the next part

of the cleaning ritual. First I use a large bath towel and go over the body to get all the spots the towel boys missed so there won't be any streaks or water stains. Next, I use Brawny paper towels and streakless Windex on the windows; Brawny leaves the least amount of lint. I also wipe the rubber window guards so I can roll the window down without messin' 'em up. Now the dust cloth is next, and I use that to apply a thin layer of Armorall to the seats, dashboard, steering wheel, and door panels. Last, I hit the rims with Ajax brass and chrome cleaner to make my joints shine like the ice on J.D.'s wrist. Then it's time to get back to land of the eternal shine.

I double-park in front of T&J Jeweler and scan the area for the ticket patrol, then jog across the street to the bank for a large deposit and light withdrawal for the day. The large crowd that usually floods 25th has slowly begun to form, and I know I gotta hurry up and make moves before everybody and they momz comes out.

I enter T&J's and behind the display counter is Ted, my man and favorite jeweler. Ted is 6 3", 240 pounds with a smile that can make any one laugh, and he's got the heart of gold. We met about five years ago in front of a club called the Sports Bar. I was peepin' this money-green 525 Benz with dark-green interior, smoky-green tints and BBS rims with a teddy bear in the middle. He walked over and started tellin' me about the car and while we kicked it, of course we knew a lot of the same people, and came to find out both our momz were from the same town upstate. And the nigga's birthday is the day before mine. The next year Ted and I hung out so much people thought we were brothers. The year after that, we had the party at Club 21 and that's when I met Ebony. Two months earlier, Ted met Gwen, and her and Eb ended up being as close as me and Ted.

"What up?"

"Yo, your piece is ready. And I must admit, my skills is right." He removes a small box from under the counter, places it on the showcase and opens it revealing the 5-inch diamond chipped outlined Nefrititi head. "Yeah Ted. No doubt, no doubt." He removes her counterpart the 18-inch figaro link and merges the perfect combination before handing it to me like a newborn baby. It catches the sun's rays and sends them in my direction, causing me to smile in appreciation. I waste no time locking it around my neck, and I size it up in the mirror behind him. Ted, "Yo . . . I'm askin' Gwen to marry me."

"Say word, when?"

"As soon as the ring is ready."

"My nigga, Big Ted Boogie, getting married." I give my man crazy love across the counter. "Yeah and you know what . . . I'm diggin' it too. I'm crazy nervous though. I hope she'll say yes –she will –she better. I'm sayin', we talked about it a while ago and she said she'd like to be married."

"You sure you doin' the right thing?"

"Yo V, I ain't never been more sure of anything in my life. Yo, what's up with you and Eb?"

"We're all good. Lately I been thinkin' 'bout doin' the same thing but . . . I'm sayin' really –I'm stallin' for what I don't even know."

"You got a great woman, dog, and you better do the right thing." Suddenly, everything becomes clear. I should have done this a long time ago. Then with unnerving calmness, "Yo, you right kid . . . Let me see the rings." Ted's right. Ebony is damn near perfect, and it's time for me to settle down and start building a foundation. She deserves to be with someone who'll love her forever. Honestly, I have no doubt about marrying her, none whatsoever, so what the hell has been stopping me. I don't even want to look at another woman, and there's not a day that goes by when I don't want to be with her.

Ted leads me over to the engagement rings and shows me the one he ordered for Gwen; it has a slim band with four gold strips holding a boulder. "Damn Ted! She can't say no to a joint like that. How much was it?"

"Sales priced at $12,000 but with my hookup, only 2."

"2! For all that, damn. What kind a hookup you got?"

"Yo, don't ask me no questions and I ain't got to tell you no lies."

"I damn sure ain't got 12 g's for a ring. I'm sayin' I'm doin' aiight on the job but-"

"Come on nigga, I ain't chargin' you the sales price doggy. You my muthafuckin' man. All you gotta do is give me a down payment of 500 and Eb's ring size, and I'll handle the rest."

"Aiight, can you give me a wider band and put "To Ebony with love" inside? And she's a size 7. Here and put it on my card."

"Can you believe it, me and you getting married . . . Yo,

how 'bout we ask them together. We can take them to *Tavern On The Green* and get an orchestra for a sucka for love feel."

"Yeah! And after dinner we'll take 'em on the lawn area with the lights n' shit."

"Or how 'bout we take 'em on the *Spirit of New York*. They got an orchestra."

"Better yet, let's go out to dinner tonight and we'll spark a convo about it and let 'em run their mouths so we can get and idea of what they'll like."

"Aiight, meet me in front of my building like 8:30."

"Aiight. Yo good lookin' on the ring too."

"No doubt." I walk out of T&J's feeling like a million dollar man, I think I'm more excited about this than Ebony will be. Me and Ted getting engaged, I never would've thought –I feel like I'm speedin'—work is goin' goo. Marriage is around the corner. I feel like I'm on top of the world. My best friend's fiancée is crazy close to my fiancée—who could ask for more.

I hop in the Ac feelin' like Hannibal when he con- quered those crackers. Ebony is going to hate me for sur- prising her like this but –Oh! Before I go any further I gotta consult the all-knowing guru of love. I pick up the cell and punch in seven digits, "Hello Ma, it's me. Listen to this."

"What?"

"I put down on a ring for Ebony."

"About time. It sure took you long enough." I look at the phone puzzled; expected a different response, "Ma' you don't think I'm speedin'?"

"Boy please! She's seen you more than I have in the last

two years. You two were made for each other. She'll be so happy. We were startin' to believe you weren't going to ask her."

"We? What we? Who? You and Ebony, we?"

"Yeah, I wanted you to ask her a long time ago. Who you think made the decision to start moving her clothes into your apartment?"

"What! Ma you set me up?"

"Oh please. If it wasn't for me, you may have ended up with another one of those fatal attraction girls; be happy Ebony came to me for help."

"I don't believe it, you and Ebony –Ma you supposed to be on my side."

"I am, that's why I helped her. Yeah well anyway, it's for your own goo. So are you and Ebony comin' to dinner tomorrow? I'm makin' chicken."

"Yeah, we'll be there."

"Look DaVon, don't be cheap. When you ask her, make sure you go all out, so she'll have a beautiful memorable moment."

"I will. See you tomorrow." I should've known–all my life my momz has nudged me in the direction she thought I should go. Me and momz always been close, not best friends, but we've got a close mother-son relationship. My father didn't participate in raising me and my brothers so momz and I always depended on each other. She instilled in me everything I needed to become what I am and she never criticized my mistakes because she knew I would learn from them, and she always stuck by me in everything.

I always discussed my plans with her, and if I didn't, she understood it was something I wanted to do on my own. Even when I didn't ask her for help, she managed to still push me in the right direction. It's obvious my mother has been training Ebony to know what we want and need, and how to get me to do what she wants me to do without me putting up a fuss. But on the real, I don't mind. It ain't like they don't love me.

Levels is located on 125ᵗʰ right off Morningside Ave. There's a big red awning that separates it from the rest of the stores in that area. The décor also gives the impression that this is more than just a barbershop. The parquet floors and antique mirrors combined with the comfortable and exquisite leather sofa and barber chairs makes it a meeting place as well as a hair sculpting center. A lot of people don't realize that, like the people in Harlem, the best barbershops are less flashy and barely seen. Every Saturday, this block is filled with all the chosen vehicles of the young, gifted and well-off men of New York like: Navigators, 4x4's, Lex coupes, Toyota Celicas, Cadillac Devilles, Accords, and of course, AC coupes.

As usual, the barbershop is not packed because the appointments make it so, yet every chair is occupied with regulars. There's a heated debate goin' on. The door closes behind me alerting the crowd of a newcomer and immediately I'm asked, "Yo Von, who you think got the better crossover, Allen Iverson or Jordan in his rookie year?" I look at him like he asked what color Eb's eyes are, and the whole shop waits in silence like I'm EF Hutton, "Hell yeah.

Iverson's shit is better." Everyone explodes into a roar like the New York Stock Exchange. Just another day in Levels. Kazo puts the finishin' touches on a young woman's dark ceasar and, "Yo the picnic's still on for next weekend right?" I ask.

Kay says, "Hell yeah. The only way it'll be canceled is if it rains."

Jay says, "We didn't cancel last year."

Kay says, "That's 'cause it rained while we were there. That was crazy as hell too. Yo, we was playin' football when it started rainin' and niggas just kept playin'. Then Ray set it off. Little Troy was on our team and the nigga scored like four times 'cause no one could hold him; we was playin' three-second hold. So Sed threw a short pass and Troy shook like five niggas and Ray came out of nowhere and clocked his little ass. Knocked him right into a mud puddle, after that –niggas just went wild. Von's girl got it all on tape too, you still got it?"

"Yeah –I'll bring by Thursday night."

"Don't front again, every time you say you comin' through, you front." Says Jay.

"Aiight, I'll make sure I come through on Thursday." Kazo brushes the cut hair from the neck of the chic with the ceasar, and whips the nylon sheet from around him. A young guy about 16 gets up preparin' to take a seat when Kazo says, "He's next Daddy-O; he called. He had an appointment." The kid sits back down extremely disappointed and, "Don't worry youngblood, one day you'll get hip and do the same thing."

Kazo begins my hair sculpting process with the precision and skill of a surgeon, out lining my edges to a razor sharpness and shaping my blow-out to utter perfection. The blow out is a masterpiece in itself; it's just a modified version of the afro. Harlem cats gotta look neat and presentable so we've made it exceptionally precise. First, a moisturizer is applied to the hair so it won't be dried out when blow-dried and picked out. Hence the name blow-out. My blow-out is cut flat across the top and rounded on the sides and back, givin' it an asymmetrical shape. Kazo also makes sure to taper the back because he knows I like to wear the collar up on my leathers, and we can't have it distort the perfection he has created. The temples and around the ears are tapered as well because I've been known to wear sunglasses, and again, he can't have one of his masterpieces twisted and representin' Levels. Kazo continues to astound me as he swings the chair around so I can shine from his gift. No matter how many times Kay blesses me, he never ceases to amaze me. And finally for the piece de resistance he laces me with the hair sheen to add the sparklin' superstar effect.

As I take one last look at my picture-perfect sight, one of Harlem's finest, Jess, explodes into the shop with two cases of Champagne and a stack of paper cups and, "Yo niggas, I just had a 10-pound baby boy." The cheers of congratulations are joined by the explosion of poppin' corks. Jess hands out and niggas start pourin' the White Star and I yell, "Yo, yo let's make a toast. To the next generation of Harlem's finest and superstars." It seems like just yesterday when Jess told us he was havin' a baby and we had a party in the shop for him. I've known this nigga since I been comin' to the shop, and I'm sayin', even though our friendship doesn't go further than Levels events, I still feel like he's fam. Really we all family. We let our kids get their cuts here. We bring our girlfriends and wives to all the parties and functions, and when there's women or kids in the shop, all the cursing and use of the word "nigga" are brought to such a minimum it's almost nonexistent. We always respect our people in the shop, like it says we function in Levels.

Back in the Ac, visions of me and Eb on our wedding day fill my mind. I still can't believe I'm makin' weddin' moves. I never saw myself bein' married –I never imagined myself— raisin' a family . . . A family, the one thing I've been runnin' from since I was 13 finally happened. A nigga has grown up. For so long I been runnin' from headaches that come with adulthood. But it's all good 'cause there's a side that makes it all worth it, the love and happiness side. Being in love and raising seeds is the next level, and I really need to stop running from it and embrace it. I wait at the light and a squeaky voice invades, "Hey Von." Damn chickens. The Ac is attacked by three neighborhood chics who've made it their goal in life to snag a nigga who'll take of them.

The head chicken is Meeka, "What's up Von?" she says as she leans in the driver's window crowded by her little sister and chicken-in-trainin' Quita, "Where you goin'? Can we get a ride?" I see these two almost everywhere Uptown, and every time I do –they're doin' the same thing; tryin' to put some cat in the dope fiend. Meeka been throwin' herself at me since I moved on the block, and in the last few months, she put her little sister under her wing for backup. "Von where ya girl at?" asks Meeka.

"I'm 'bout to pick her up right now."

"Why you keep frontin' on Meeka Von? You know she tryin' to see you." Says Quita. I shake my head at the tackiness that surrounds me. "Von I don't care about your girl, if you don't. I just-"

"Where yo' kids at Meeka?"

"They're at my mother's house."

"Don't you think you should be with them?"

"Why can't you just stop frontin' boo? Nobody gotta know. You can come through on the late night."

"How I'ma creep with you when you got three or four other niggas doin' the same thing?"

"If you come through, all that'll change."

"Oops green light, gotta go."

I feel sorry for Meeka. The father of her first baby caught a body in D.C and she ended up replacing him with the father of her second child who managed to get twisted back on his way home from the gamblin' spot. She never did bounce back from that. She always depended on them to take care of her mentally and physically and they did. Now that they're gone she's desperate, she'll take anything a nigga puts her in as long as he acts right.

One night, not long after I moved on the block, I was sittin' in Morning Side Park lacin' my taste buds with the all, mighty Hen-rock. Meeka stepped in my Henny-induced haze and sat on the next bench over. She peeped I was new on the block so she hit me with the verbals, and just 'cause

I'm a cool nigga, I invited her to get saucey. Quickly, the Hen-rock took effect and she began telling me about her past relationships, and what brought her to this Hen-rock-filled scene. Buss how her second baby's father's man was helping her with the kids. Doe, pampers—eventually she started messin' with Money. Then she found out he had two other chics and both of them got kids by him, and she still stayed with him. Of course, I wanted to know why and, "Because he takes care of me." I damn sure couldn't understand that. As time passed, I kept seeing her around the block, and I'd always listen to her sorted love twist and try to advise her. Eventually she wanted to get with me, but she's got way too much drama goin' on in her life.

Meeka does whatever it takes to have someone hold her at night and make her feel safe and warm, even if it's an illusion which only lasts one night. Ebony hated her, but she didn't see the pain in her eyes when she told me those stories. She didn't see the woman who didn't know how to get what she wanted the right way. Too bad my whole zone is tainted by the lost souls of twisted ghetto love.

With great amazement, I find a space on 25th across the street from *Beauty Now*, and I prepare myself. I'm about to enter the realm of "burn it, cut it to make me beautiful for him." I cross the threshold and, as if they felt the presence of an intruder, every woman under a dryer looks at me. I feel like a Crip in Blood territory. I proceed to the styling area trying not to pay attention to the hot torture chambers as I pass them. Ebony is sitting in a chair as Nisha, her beautician and my ex-high school sweetheart, fusses with the rollers. Nisha and I were in deep like/lust our senior year of high school, and she's still my peoples. One night, Ebony needed an emergency touchup for a party we were goin' to and when her beautician was unavailable I came to the rescue. Eventually through what was an undercover interrogation of Nisha, Ebony found out we had a brief history. From that day on, Eb's been goin' to Nisha to get her hair done. I don't know if it's 'cause she digs her work or because she wants to keep an eye on her.

As I close in on them, Nisha looks at me and smiles and whispers something top secret to Eb. They were talking about me. I've been around enough women to be able to tell. Nisha, "Hiii Vony." She's the only one who can call me that, "What up Nish?"

"Hey boo, gimme a kiss," Ebony says with her hand extended. I follow orders and notice how she's still sexy as hell with rollers in her hair. "Where's the piece?" Asks Ebony. I open my jacket so the golden diamond studded Queen Nefrititi can shine, "Ooo that's pretty booby, I might have to get a King Tut like that so we can click. What you think Nish?"

"I like it, he always knows how to do his thing without goin' too far, but you and King Tut—don't think so. Maybe a lion's head, that fits him –a lion's head." They start laughin' hysterically and it's obvious they've been talking about me, probably something about sex. "How much longer Nish?"

"All I gotta do is take out these rollers and make sure it's dry enough to style."

"So what—about an hour?"

"No! Half tops."

"Aiight, I'm goin' to the fish spot. You want somethin' Eb?"

"Shrimp platter."

"What about you Nish?"

"Shrimp platter too." I breeze off, thinking about a nice crispy fish sandwich on wheat bread and tartar sauce with a big cup of half and half. The fish spot is on the corner of the block and just like every Saturday afternoon the line ain't nothin' to fuck with. 125th and Madison is my favorite fish spot after the Crab Inn and one of the many places where one of my ex-girls happens to work.

Before Ebony and I became an official couple, I flirted with and/or dated chics who worked in a spot where I wanted a hookup: like clothing stores, jewelry stores, electronic stores, movie theaters, token booths, toll booths, the post office, Motor Vehicles, airlines, travel agencies, grocery stores, and especially, the phone company. And to ensure I'd be able to benefit from their service, I always ended the relationship on good terms. The places where I wasn't datin' someone I made sure to douse the clerk or clerks with a thick coat of venomous flirting to help bring customer friendliness to a new level. It got to a point where my peoples were getting hookups on the strength of me. Once my mother had her car towed for parking in a red zone and she went to the impound to pay the $50 ticket plus the $300 for the towing fee. When she got there, she saw this chic I used to mess with. Now she only saw shorty one time and she almost didn't remember who she was, yet shorty blessed her, and my momz only had to pay the $ 50 ticket.

Another time, I invited one of my peoples and three of her friends over—I was cookin' that night. We chilled and got saucy all night. A month later, I took my little brothers to a Knicks' game at *The Garden.* They won that night. One of the women who came with my peoples saw me and we kicked it for a minute. Come to find out she's the head of the liaison committee for *The Garden,* buss how she took us from the almost nosebleed seats to two rows from courtside at half court, and! She got both my brothers official game balls signed by Spreewell, Allan, and L.J. Even though I didn't get with her or try to, my regular, respectable nice guy behavior helped us to shine nicely. It also allowed me to show my little brothers how important it is to be nice even if she's not your girl. To help you truly feel the depth of my skillz here's one last story.

Early in our relationship, Ebony and I had dinner at one of those seafood spots on City Island and the maitre d' was the sister of one of my former lovers who was, unknown to me, the manager of the restaurant. That night we got a table in the executive area and we didn't pay for the lobster dinner, just as a small acknowledgment of a small portion of my worth. I was with my girl and my ex blessed us. I think about that for a minute. Ebony had a problem with the multitude of women who continued to pay me for the mental, physical, and spiritual pleasure I have once given them, until I began paying her for her wealth with my own.

I stand at the end of the line, scan the area behind the counter, and low and behold, here comes Lacy speedin' out the kitchen with an order in hand. Lacy and I had a summer thing, and it ended up with us being part-time lovers during the winter. Every time we saw each other somewhere unexpectedly we ended up wakin' up together. Eventually our situation began to lose its thrill, and we drifted apart, and now when I see her, she looks at me with those hypnotic sexy eyes and tells me to call after 12— booty call hours.

In order to fully benefit from this situation, I gotta move strategically. I don't approach the counter because it'll seem as if I'm speakin' to her to use her for whatever. Lacy is funny that way, she always wants to feel as if she has the upper hand over me or doing me a favor 'cause she knows she's helpless when I want to get my way. I hold my position and make casual eye contact, givin' her my mind-melting smile. This causes a return smile and a come-talk-to-me wave; of course I front, then she insists. Nonchalantly, I approach and we engage in simple formalities, how you doin', how's everything, why don't you call etc. etc. etc. Then she asks me for my order, and she floats off looking back to make sure I'm watching—I am 'cause I know it'll make her feel good. A hot minute later, she returns and starts baggin' the order. I try to pay but, "You can pay me back when I see you on the late night." She gets the smile and a stroke on the chin for the added finesse. On the low I do the same thing to Ebony, and she said she peeps it but for some reason she's not immune to the venomous flow that intoxicates at will. Now some people may feel like I used Lacy, but understand all I did was ask her in a different way.

Ebony hops in the Ac and we situate ourselves in preparation for our ride to the Yonkers Mall. The necessary music is set up and Eb puts a towel across her lap and seat for the accidental spills. We swing across 24th to avoid the traffic of the afternoon shoppers and get on the F.D.R. to the Major Deegan. This is when the Ac is at its best. The comfort of the bucket seats ensures a relaxing ride and the silence that engulfs the inner carriage combined with the CD is straight up studio mode. Eb tucks a napkin into my shirt to protect the Fruity from tartar sauce, then she begins to feed me, takin' her time to wipe the sauce from the corners of my mouth. She's sitting at an angle so she can be closer to me while she babies me. Her skirt reveals her thighs, and as always, I'm on the armrest with the right hand on her leg.

The ride to the mall is only 45 minutes if you're in rush, but I have no intentions of shortening this moment with Ebony. I live for these days with her when nothing else exists but us, and if I could be as close to her as I want, we'd be sharin' the same breath. Periodically our eyes meet when she gives me a bite and those split seconds seem to be lifetimes. Ebony loves to smile when she looks at me, and every time she's caressing my soul, we've somehow become one person, one force in the form of uncontested love. I drift off for a minute thinking about the ring, and she brings me back with a gentle nudge to remind me to finish the sandwich. Our eyes meet again and she gives me a heavenly stardust smile, and right at that moment, I realize there's no way I can live without this Queen of pure loveliness. I want to ask her the big question—I have to—I can't wait for the ring, "Ebony do you wanna-" then like a lightning bolt hit me, my momz's voice,

"*Von make it an unforgettable moment.*" "Do you want to . .
.mmm-move in with me?" She puts the sandwich up to my
mouth and I take a bite, then with a cool calm collectiveness that could make people in hell happy and she says,
"Yes," as if I asked if she liked my shirt. I feel like she's has
been waiting for me to ask that. Somehow I think my
mother has something to do with this. I'm not sure but this
has her m.o. all over it. There's a content silence between
us which is refreshing and reassuring because we both know
that our relationship has moved on to the next level.

We enter the mall and proceed with our normal agenda.
Like so many things we do together, we've mastered the art
of shopping. We've figured out no outfit is complete without
the proper footwear. It can make the outfit or have you
lookin' like a uncoordinated disaster. So we hit *Nine West*.
As usual, I'm the only man in the store. At one time I too
hated the thought of shopping with a woman, but I realized
I had no choice. So instead of being an innocent bystander,
I decided to be a participant. Two heads always move faster
than one. We part going to the appropriate section to pick
and choose and then meet up to get the opinion of the other.
I've been shopping with enough women to be trusted to pick
out something for Ebony. Immediately something catches my
eye, a suede forest-green-slip-on with a one-inch heel and
open toe. Women's feet are extremely attractive—at times,
more attractive then their naked sexual organs. Ebony also
has perfect size 5 feet. She can make just about any shoe look
good. Above the green ones are a burgundy heelless new
buck with white trim. She'll definitely like these. I rush over

to her showing her the green shoe first, "That's cute." Then I show her, her favorite color and, "Ooo that's niiiice." 'Cause she's hypnotized by the softness of its color. With the swiftness she hits the clerk with her size, and she returns in commission-needing time. Eb tries them on . . . suddenly I hear—no I feel a force pulling me towards the door.

I breeze outside not understanding or resisting the uncontrollable urge that pulls me. I stand in front of *Nine West* and my eyes are drawn to a store across the way. Helplessly I walk inside like a zombie being called from the grave. The smell of ripe new leather fills me and I feel like Laura running through the field on "Little House On The Prairie." I begin searching the racks for the force that— mmm. A motorcycle jacket—with a collar? It's black in the front with racing patches. The sleeves are red and black, and it's got a cream and black collar. It smiles at me and whispers, "I was made for you." And I answer, "Indeed you were." I remove it from its hanger with as much pride and glory as King Arthur did when he found Excalibur. As I slide it on, its thickness softens just a bit to form with my slim frame. The extra stiff collar has risen to the occasion as if it knew I rocked like that. The fit is well tailored and this white Fruity and chain set off the complete ensemble as if made for each other. Ebony enters after I'm well into the fifth minute of admiring my new appendage and, "Buy it boo. You look so good in leathers. Those broad shoulders is what does it." A young female clerk who's around 17 and dewy eyed approaches. She looks so innocent, a little too innocent, dangerously innocent. Like she can get a nigga to do whatever she wants –good or bad, partners in crime type shit.

Shorty says, "You're the only one who looked that good in this jacket since I've been here. I've talked three guys out of buying it because I didn't think they would respect the power of it. But you—I think you do." Yeah Shorty's dangerous. "You guys married?"

Ebony says, "Not yet." I act like I don't hear her.

"We have a skirt that matches that jacket. It's only in one size, and I think you're it," Says Shorty She shows her a thigh high sleeveless low cut leather skirt that zips up in front from the waist. It's red with black trim and has black patches. Eb disappears into the dressing room as I continue to feel myself in the leather I merged with. Minutes later, Ebony returns and—Damn! She looks crazy sexy. It's a perfect fit, hugging in just the right places. She walks over to the mirror, examines herself and says, "What chu think?"

"What I think?" I'm momentarily silent, looking for the right words to express the sexual craving I've received after seeing her in that dress. "I'm feelin' that dress more than my karate movies." She looks at shorty and, "We'll take 'em."

We continue to follow our plan and look for shirts and blouses, as we . . . "What's that smell Eb?"

"What smell?"

"I think—that perfume—it smells like . . ." We look at each other and say, "*Victoria's Secret.*" Our favorite store. Every man in America with a beautiful girlfriend, lover, fiancée, or wife should be thankful and applaud the splendor of satin that *Victoria* has to offer. The store is filled with the soft aroma of their special perfume, a scent I'm sure no man can resist or ignore. Like I said, Ebony is not too fond of panties, and I know this sounds ill, but it used to be a problem. I love the female anatomy, hers in particular, and I love satin panty and bra sets more than nakedness. Being that Ebony hated to be restricted, we had to compromise. We decided negligees and teddies would suit both our needs. She could be satinized without being restricted, and Victoria has a wide variety of both. We continue to search the silk and satin pleasure palace picking sexually inciting garments, then Eb wants to try a few on. Now she likes to surprise me when we pick out joints for her, but a lot of times I manage to sneak a peek while she's trying them on. The way the dressing rooms are set up a nigga, can get a look if he wants too. Sometimes the attendants be tryin' to throw salt in my game so I hold a couple of items and stand near the entrance. But—Eb's hip so, "Von."

"Yeah."

"Get away from the dressing room."

"I'm sayin', I was gonna hand you something to try on."

"That's what the lady is for." Damn, deaded again.

I carry the Victoria's Secret bag with a silent excitement in anticipation of what she's going to look like. I think she sensed my burning desire to see her in the beauty that Vicki had blessed us with, and in attempts to hold down the sexual monster, she slides her hand in mine. Slowly a warmth that can only come from love seeps through my pores like the Ebola virus and attacks my bloodstream sending an energy through me that fills my soul with . . . love.

We walk pass a jewelry counter and Eb stops and again I feel like I've fallen into another one of my mother's well-woven webs 'cause Eb ain't never looked at engagement rings. She carefully studies each one and then, "Ooo look at this one. Von isn't that pretty?" I say nothing as I inspect it. It's half the size of the one I chose and the band is thinner, "You really like that? It's crazy cheesy, look at that skinny band—looks like somethin' out of a bubble gum machine."

"I'm sayin, it's nice for the price."

"Fuck a price. If you gonna buy an engagement ring, you mind as well go all out. Who wants to look at a lame ass ring-." Oh no, don't fall for that one kid, my mother's been trainin' her, but she's not a pro yet. I better end this one before I blow everything.

"So you buyin' me a ring?"

"What? Come on shorty keep it movin'. I need some new games. I said move in not marry." Nice try but not yet.

The day slowly becomes night. We ended our shopping excursion early 'cause doe is too low to be in the mall all day. We relax on the couch in our regular position, Eb sits with one leg on the couch and the other on the coffee table while I rest my head on her lap. She begins playing in my hair and asks, "What are we havin' for dinner?"

"Oh, I forgot Ted and Gwen invited us to dinner, you wanna cancel?"

"No, I haven't seen Gwen in awhile. What time?"

"eight-thirty,"

"Good, that gives us a few hours to cool out." The more she twirls, the heavier my eyes become and slowly I feel myself slipping into a dream state. I feel like a child being rocked to sleep in the arms of someone protective and loving, a feeling I will soon forget ever existed.

I'm awakened by a gentle hand caressing my cheek and an angelic voice calling my name, I wait for the angel to appear because only a dream could sound so beautiful. The voice continues and, "I need my leg back so I can get dressed." She whispers. I even love the way she wakes me up. Sometimes she kisses me just as I open my eyes. I close my eyes and clutch her thigh tighter, in refusal. "Come on booby, it's already seven, I have to find something to wear. I finally release what I have had my lips on so many times, and she disappears into my—correction our bedroom. I figure since I've got like an hour to kill, I might as well crack open NBA Live 2001 and have the Knicks scrape the Pacers the way they always should've done. As always, while I'm catching wreck on the Playstation, I'm thinkin' about what I'ma wear, since I just got my chain back. I'll go all black tonight. Black slacks, mock neck tee shirt and leather shirt which helps the Queen Nefrititi to shine in her wintery setting. "Von where we goin' tonight?"

"How about The Butta Lounge? They got a jazz band on Saturdays."

"What about that place on West End Ave. *The Suga Café.*"

"Aiight." I forgot to tell Ted the plans so he'll be appropriately dressed so I hit his mobile and leave a message.

Just like clockwork, Eb comes swaying by in a mustard skirt with a thigh-high split and matching shoes and just a bra while putting on her earrings and, "That's the new game you bought?"

"Yeah."

"You gonna teach me to play this one?"

"You ain't ready for this."

"You said that about the 2000 too, and I beat you 2 times for the title."

"That's because I felt sorry for you and let you win."

"Von."

"What?"

"Turn off the game and get dressed."

"Yes mommy dearest." I move to the closet, and in less than 30, I'm almost ready when I decide to take a few minutes extra to make sure the blowout is as perfectly shaped as it was when I left *Levels*. Ebony comes in while I'm taking that last look and stands in front of me and rests her hands on my waist, looks into my eyes, and I can see the happiness in her. It's as if there's no words to describe her feelings. All she can say is, "I love you." That time she penetrated my soul.

"I love you too."

"One day, Von, your gonna let me be your wife and love you forever."

"You right."

Ted lives 15 minutes away and as we pull up to his building. Gwen is the first to appear. Her leather-fitted pants with mini DKNY shirt cling to her 55-150-pound frame, to show her flare for semi-glamour. In a way, she reminds me of Ebony. They both have the same natural beauty; neither of them wears makeup except for the occasional lipstick. Gwen is just a bit more snappy and a lot thicker. Ted walks behind her completely overshadowing her. She looks like a child next to him, really everyone looks like a child next to him. For a big guy I must say my man wears his fits well. Most big guys don't pay attention to the fit of their clothes, but those beige pants and matching silk shirt definitely let my man breathe and shine.

Gwen and Eb haven't seen each other in awhile, and they insist on sitting in the back to discuss top-secret classified information that we're not authorized to hear.

Our ride across Riverside is coated with a thick layer of the new DJ Clue starring the Infamous B.B.O. niggas. We hit West End and make moves to *The Suga Café*. The restaurant is a small, cozy, culturally-decorated, well-placed, down-low spot. We enter, as always, commanding star-like attention. Ted looks like a possible runningback for some team with his *Essence* magazine girlfriend, and I'm the poster boy for *Perfect Hair Inc.* with the ninth wonder of beauty by my side. The four of us take our place at a table revealing to the world what upwardly mobile, beautiful, black loving couples look like and everyone seems to be taking notes.

Unlike our soon to be fiancées, our classified communication consists of simple sentence fragments. "Yo you gonna handle that?" Asks Ted.

"No doubt." As if the business was meaningless which won't arouse any suspicion between our girls. Ted decides to make it happen first and says, "Yo, today this young chic comes in the shop wantin' to trade in a name chain. She tells me her boyfriend bought it for her because she told him a story about how someone snatched the first one she ever had and he thought it would be a nice present. Now, she wants to trade it in and get another chain. I asked her if she thought the chain meant something and if money would be mad about her getting rid of it. She looked at me like I was speakin' Chinese. My man does something every woman always says niggas don't do enough of and this chic acts like it ain't nothin' to her. Crazy ungrateful." Perfect no-look pass by Ted, now watch this 360 windmill dunk.

"Yo I was watchin' some talk show and there was this kid who asked this chic to marry him right on the stage and she said no. Then when the host asked her why, she said because that wasn't the way she wanted to be asked. Then she went into some 'ole 'Days Of Our Lives' proposal shit."

"So!—I would've said no too, if she told him how she wanted it to be then he should of did it," Says Gwen.

"She never told him anything. He was tryin' to surprise her. How was he supposed to know she wanted some *Alice in Wonderland* shit."

"He should've known proposing on stage on TV lacks imagination. He could've thought of something better," says Ebony.

"Yeah, he probably was just too cheap to do anything else." Says Gwen. Then just as expected, they begin tossing ideas between each other about what a memorable proposal would be. Ted and I end up getting more info than we planned. Now we have a game plan. All we gotta do is make it happen. Ted and I are flamboyant experts so believe we'll be pullin' off a historical tear jerkin', "All My Children,"

"Young And The Restless," session finale, cliff-hanging proposal. Yeah, we about to do it up for the women we love.

Night Fall

I knew I would have to test Storm in a few things before we could pull off this jux.

First I needed to know if his trigga had any heart. When doin' a jux, it's easy to shoot a nigga who's shootin' at you, who's runnin' away, or reachin' for the heat. But if the nigga refuses to cooperate, he's gotta have no fear, no remorse. If by some chance someone sees your face, there's no way you can leave witnesses, and how hard will it be for him to twist a nigga who's unarmed or begging for his life. On my way to Storm's buildin', I think about what spot we'll hit for his first job. The hustlin' gods is supposed to hear my prayers this weekend which will give us a little more time to kick it. I sit on the stoop in front of Storm's building as the dark side's sun rises and takes over its realm. Moments later, my little man comes out wearin' the outfit I bought him the night before. I see he has no intentions of going back to his regular. "What's the deal?"

"Money nigga."

"No question. Yo, we gotta get you some new wears."

"Na. I wanna remember how it feels to be fucked up for a while. So I'll always keep my mind right." The niggas got a little "wis" with him too. He rolls up while I stand at the edge of the stoop thinkin' about what the best target would be. He suddenly looks up like a deer who's down, wind of a

*hunter. He stands up and scans the block for a moment and,
"What's up?"*

*"Na, I thought I . . . a vic. It's ill but I thought I could tell
a vic was comin'." Damn! The nigga's got it, I wanna smile
'cause . . . quickly I, too, search the block for the scent of the
prey my little man picked up. Then I look down the one way
block and a red 600 cat catches my eye. I turn back to Storm
resting my leg on the second step, and say, "Peep the 600
comin' down the block." He continues to roll while intensely
watching, "Yo nigga, I'm sayin' put some shade on that. Stalk
them niggas like the Feds." Periodically he looks at them as
they get closer, "They slowin' down, keep your hand on it just
in case. There's three—two fat dudes in the back. Ballin'
nigga's too fat to be hit men. Driver's got the gun. I can see
it in his face. They're stoppin'." I wait for his signal, I can't
afford to make a mistake and body a nigga for no reason.
Storm feels the vibe and, "Be easy they're lookin' for someone—no something. Niggas want weight." This block is full
of basement storage areas with so many ki's that coppin' is as
easy as buyin' a $ 2 bottle. Storm and I can be mistaken for
Spanish niggas on a block full of them, so it's obvious the 600
thought they could pick up somethin' from us but they're in
for a surprise.*

*They pull off and drive to the corner. Then the two pas-
sengers get out and waddle towards one of the main herr-on
distributing buildings in the zone; they're both 300 and better with Coogi sweater vest and heavy jewels. I know their
pickin' up at least 2 kilos so I figure this will be a good time
to see what my little man is made of. "Yo I'ma take care of*

the driver and move the car around the corner. If they come
out follow them and I'll find you." I walk towards the corner
planning to inspect the drivers status to see how I'm gonna
play it. At one time, my heart would be pounding through my
chest and I'd be getting a blood rush to my head simulating
a roller coaster ride. But that was when I was young and
immature. That was when I juxed to eat and have fun. That
was when I didn't know better. Now, as I stalk my prey like the
elder black panther, I am calm and patient. I think quicker
and with more precision which prevents mistakes. No longer
does my prey manage to escape. No longer do I leave the
scene hungry for more. No longer am I seen by some clown
watchin' from afar. And no longer am I spotted by my vic,
because I am—The Red Silence of Harlem.

As I walk by, I ice grill money—sizin' up his shit. The
nigga's heavy head noddin' and he returns a defense grill.
Stupid muthafucka. I can see money's new to this game. H,e
ain't even on point. And 'cause of it, I'ma get his ass. When
a nigga comes to do dirt, you supposed to try to keep as much
beef away as possible. You don't invite it just because you
holdin'. I step to the phone on the corner, drop in a quarter,
and play telephone games—I know he's watchin' me so I
avoid eye contact. I scan the area, then walk back past him
still avoiding eye contact. Six cars away, I transform like
Decept—the stockin' cap goes over the face—the hat flips
back, and the hamma is unleashed. I breeze along the edges
of the building stayin' out of sight of the car mirror. Then I
cross into the street, two cars away. Just as I mold the cars
with my back—tire level, I realize I didn't check to see if the

doors were locked. They shouldn't be, if they had to make a fast getaway they'd have problems, rule one as a getaway, driver—leave the doors open for your crew, but he's an amateur so fuck it. My creepin' skills are excellent. He didn't even see me comin', "Get the fuck out."

"Oh shit—damn." He gets out and I frisk him and toss his gun into the sewer and his mint in my pocket. Then, just to let him know the shit was real I pistol whip him a few times. I drag his ass to his hidin' spot, "Pop the trunk and get in." I hop in the driver's seat and skirt off to the Ave. parking the car out of sight. Then I return to camouflage mode—to prevent suspicion, I head back to the phone which my vics'll have to pass in order to get to where they think their car is. I rest the heat in the fold of the arm that's holdin' the phone and it disappears from sight, can't have the number-one "hatas" in America fuckin' with my flow. While lookin' over my shoulder for my vics, I see Storm leavin' the stoop—what's he— he's movin' into a back-up position, the same thing I would've done if not given orders.

The two fat boys are takin' too long. I can out wait 'em, but I don't want Storm to get antsy and blow shit up; just then, the two come waddlin' out the buildin' empty-handed. Either they were told to come back or didn't get anything. If they're gonna come back, we've got a problem. They get closer and I have to make a decision. I look in their faces for disappointment and try to read their lips for a signal, but I get nothin'. They're almost in position and I'm about to let the whole thing ride when the shorter one says, "Fuckin' German niggas." Got 'em. I transform again and spin with the heat exposed, *"You know the deal big boy make it quick."* They look for their back-up and, *"I already got his stupid ass in the trunk, once more give it up."* The shorter one reaches into his pocket and pulls out a knot in a rubber band and tosses it to me. I look down and it's only about five thousand. Now see—he's insultin' my skill and intelligence—can't he tell I been doin' this—like I don't know how heavy 5 is and I don't know this wouldn't even get 'em in the door of the spot. My peripheral vision picks up Storm walkin' across the street pistol pointed head level of the shortest one. He maneuvers through the cars, steps onto the curve and **PHHH—PHHH** two to the head of fat man who thought I was stupid. The other one was frozen by the splatter of blood across his face, but seconds later, he was pullin' out a large envelope from his waist and hands it to me. Storm was seen by the vic and I realize he didn't care, but I do, we're a team now and if he's got beef—I got beef and we can't afford to not be able to walk the streets as we please. In his defens,e he's still young and I'll let him know so he won't make that mistake again. But for now, I have to clean up his spilt milk, so **PHHH—PHHH**, the fat man had to fall.

Due to the death that was beyond my control, the abandoned buildin' where I sometimes stash my shit after a heist is unavailable, and I found a new spot that same night. Storm and I split up the money, includin' the two knots they tried to front with, and I ask him, *"What you gonna do with the doe?"*

"First I'ma get a piece for the Cuban Nonye gave me, then I'ma go shoppin', give my grandmother a little somethin', and stack the rest."

"*Good, have fun with it and find a chic to splurge with, fuck the niggas on the block.*"

"*I already found one.*"

"*Who, Nonye? I'm sayin', she's aiight. She'll take care of a nigga who does the right thin. Just don't be fuckin' no low-budget bitches around the block, and keep crazy shade on your shit. She won't stress it too much 'cause you still young, but if you cheat on her, it better be with a chic like her or better . . . Yo, next time get a stockin' cap so you don't gotta keep killin' niggas. It's bad for business. Why you come across the street and twist money?*" He pauses while lookin' at his money then looks at me and says, "*I could tell he was bullshittin' and stallin' and I kinda figured you'd pistol whip money before blastin' him. That right there would've made him start yellin' and there was an open window right above my head and I heard voices. So to stop muthafuckas from callin' the police, I had to keep shit quiet. I know it's better to pull shit off without bodies, but this time it would've caused problems.*" His calmness makes him interesting and it's almost like he was learnin' some shit as he thought about the whole thing. I wish I could spend more time with Shorty so I could see his face when I give him jewels to further his career. In a way I'd be able to relive my youth in a kid who ain't my own. Too bad it has to be on the dark side.

$ $ $ $ $ $ $

The money we got from the fat boys was a nice start for Storm but only shoppin' money for me and my son, and it's

not enough for the supplies for my last heist. The hustlin'
gods answered my prayers for this weekend and today is a
nice night for me to test Storm once again. The gamblin' spots
are always bubblin' on these nights which make them a prime
target for The Red Silence and The Quiet Storm of Harlem.

I get one of the local car thieves to get a ride for the jux.
We're makin' moves out to Queens so we'll be alright for a
couple of hours. By the time the car gets hot, the shit'll be
dumped and we'll be back Uptown. For the last heist, I'll
have to get a rented and just drive it down South, then
report it stolen when I'm done. That's too long of a ride to
take a chance in a stolen car.

We pull in an alleyway across the street from this spot,
and I fill my little man in, "There's a bathroom in the back
room where the big-dog card game is goin' on. We can
climb down the fire escape right into the bathroom window.
There'll probably be three guards, one near the entrance to
the outer club part and another near the door to the alley.
And another one floatin'. It'll be like $ 20,000 or better.
Niggas are most likely holdin' too so watch 'em. Let them
know we just hungry niggas tryin' to eat and don't take it
personal. They'll ease off and won't be too quick to chase
us. We'll leave out the alley door after takin' security's
weapons, then leave them at the bottom of the steps. We
don't need to carry anything extra."

"You got a bag for the money."

"Yeah." I look in his face, and I see the energy explod-
ing—I hope he don't develop an itchy trigga finga.

We leave the car unlocked, and I put the master ignition

key in my left glove. We make our way to the fire escape, movin' under the cover of the rain and without the dark side's sun. We ain't worryin' about police 'cause they, like everyone else in this weather, become laxed and unaware of the things that would normally grab their attention. The fire escape is on the second floor, and the ledge is wide enough to walk across—I'm about to step out on the ledge, and again, I 'm concerned about Storm's trigga finga— I put my hand on his chest and his heart is poundin' like a scared rabbit. I know it's a rush but I remind him, "Remember no bodies." He nods and his look tells he'll do his best. I step on the ledge like it ain't a three-story drop. I scale it grace- fully almost like I was a trained high-wire stunt man. I check my man who's seemingly unfazed by the drop as well. The window is open, I look inside to make sure it's clear before sliding in feet first, touching down like there was a pillow under my feet. We creep up on the door, and I'm won- dering if it creaks. I need to see how many guards there are, "Fuck it." I swing the door open, scan the room like the Terminator— counting how many guards and, "Just chill. Don't make it messy. Put the guns down slowly. Yo you first," I say to the closet one. "Now move over near your crew. You two, guns down and kick them to the side." They follow reluctantly and slowly. "Aiight, everybody keep your hands on the table where I can see 'em." There's six play- ers tonight, an average amount, "All we want is the table money, you fill up this bag." Storm keeps his eyes on every- one and he doesn't point the gun in anyone's face. Big dogs look at that like disrespect.

The head of the table hands Storm the bag and we back
away to the door, jet down the short steps and into the alley,
then across the street back to the car and.we're on our way
back Uptown with out lettin' off one shot.

The Darker Side

The next morning Red's baby's momz wakes up in one
of her normally foul moods. She makes Tyriq a bowl of
cereal and tries to pacify him with morning cartoons. Back
in the room, she gets dressed in her usual chicken-head
attire and sits on the bed to watch Red while he sleeps. He
even sleeps silently like he's awake and pretending. She
hates his slick charming charismatic ways, yet she loves
him with every inch of her being. She hates that she played
with his emotions and left him when he needed her the
most. She was too busy trying to be seen in somebody's car
or getting some nigga to buy her sneakers. She made stupid
immature mistakes, and she can't find the words to apologize, but he should know she's sorry because she lets him
stay there. She cooks for him and keeps the house clean. But
how does he know, he doesn't and he won't so fuck him-he
never wanted her anyway she thought. Pretty mothafucka.
She wants to make him mad so she decides she'll move his
little gun so he'll go crazy lookin' for it. She slides the radiator up a bit and slides her hand in the hole where he keeps
that thing he loves more than . . . wait what's this she
thought. She pulls out a brown plastic bag folded neatly.

She opens it and finds the money from the heist last night. She figures the best way to get him mad will be to spend his little money on things for the house and the baby. Maybe he'll love her more if she gets her hair and nails done.

After getting Tyriq dressed, the wannabe Mrs. The Red Silence of Harlem hurries across the street to her partner in crime's house affectionately called the "cutthroat car hoppin' hooker." They leave Tyriq and the hooker's kids at the mother's house and plan their day of spending the money she acquired from Red.

First, they hop in a cab headed for the Dominican beauty shop on 145th and St.Nick. Hours pass and the Dominicans do their best to rid the chickens of their feathers but that's like trying to get a Muslim to eat a pork chop sandwich. Back in cab—next stop 125th, then, in a blur, the money is . . . *Gone.*

3

THE BEGINNING OF THE END

The following weekend, me, my man Ted, his girl Gwen, and Ebony pile into Ted's five and a quarter headed for Roosevelt Park for the 3rd annual *Levels* picnic. Gwen and Eb are the designated drivers 'cause me and Ted are going to partake in a fine plethora, a.k.a. Courvosier.

The parking lot reserved for Levels is a straight Auto Show Scene. The gold trimmed 850 is here, the twin BMW wagons, two-door Accords, the Q45 Suvs, Lex coupes, Lexus Jeep, Suburban, Durango, Navs, Montero sports, 525, 850, 318, 500, 750, E-classes, the Z3, the Jag, Miata, even the regulators came on Dukatis and Kawasaki. Harlem's Finest have truly come out to represent. There's a blue and white banner that marks our designated area and from Big Sed's black on black Nav parked on the grass, and the sounds of the Black Assassin exploding from his speakers, we know the VIP area is nearby. Every couple of years, Sed cops a truck and when he comes through, he unofficially marks the area where the shops long-time customers will gather for drinks and convo. True—every one at the picnic is a part of the family one way or another, but the close ones, the every event attendees usually sit together. We lay our blanket in the well-sunned area, and Ted and I float around giving love to our peoples and sippin' the sauce with whoever's got a cup.

We find one of Harlem's finest, Del, under a tree with a bottle of something that resembles what we want, and we decide to join him.

"What's the word Del?" asks Ted.

"Same ole cuzin, eatin' and shinin'" says Del.

"You dolo today?"

"Na wifey breezed with my sister. I had to bring her, my girl is on some-be-mad-at Del shit for whatever I choose. My little sister'll keepin' the beef off me. How's business Von? I heard you supposed to be workin' with Def Jam on some big deal with someone special" says Del.

"Yeah, we ain't worked out the contracts yet but I got all the beats laid out for them."

"Yo I got some young kids out of Queens I want you to listen to them see if you can do something for them." Says Del.

"Aiight."

"Yo, Big Ted what's up with the shine shop?" says Del.

"I'm still payin' bills," Says Ted.

"Yo, I got some niggas from Omaha who just signed with Motown, so you know they'll be tryin' to get heavy soon. So of course I'm sendin' them to the number one jeweler in New York." Says Del.

"No question," Says Del.

"Enterprising, networking, wifeys rides and shines. Superstars and Harlem's Finest."

"Who said niggas don't make power moves?" says Del. Del holds up his cup and toasts to the pleasure and beauty of proving everyone wrong. As we enjoy the shade and liqs, three women, we all know a little too well, slide up and surround us like three Knick defenders at a Miami game. The shortest is a crazy thick 5'4 terror, her thighs and calves come from her Penn Relay trophy days. Her short cut reveals the smooth neckline leading to the cleavage that is semi covered by her Perry Ellis tank top.

"I know y'all ain't come here alone." Says Monique. The next is the sexiest and most seductive, Natalie. I was at one time easily weakened by her sensual low-toned, lightly vibrating moan, and the motion of her lips whenever she says, "What's up M&M?" She calls me M&M because she says I can make any woman strung out 'cause I make them melt with my mouth and not my hands, both verbally and . . . well . . . she doesn't mean just kissing. "What up Nat?"

"Where you been hiddin' out lately? We haven't seen or heard from our Harlem hit squad in a while. And I haven't waited up in my Victoria's Secrets for you in so long. They're getting lonely." Says Nat. Oh boy, there she goes. I hope Ebony doesn't see her. I ain't doin' anything but, you fellas know that doesn't matter. Now the third is Shay, quiet yet the most dangerous adversary of them all. Her eyes have the power of 10 snake charmers and 12 hypnotists, too powerful for the most strongest willed. There's been times when I've seen her put her spell on every one in a club, even three female bartenders . . . straight ones.

Shay says, "Yeah, we didn't see y'all at the Bad Boy ski trip, you stopped comin' through the hot spots. Y'all even missed the Greek Freak in Philly and Va, and Ted I thought you and Von would never miss homecoming at Hampton."

"And you brought your girls to the Final Four party. What's goin' on? Don't tell me ya'll niggas done threw away your Ghetto Fab cards." Says Monique.

"It ain't that Mo, I'm sayin' our status just elevated to the next level. Like you said we been there done that three four times and now it's time to move on to the next plateau." Says Ted.

"I'm sayin', why don't ya'll show us the way so we can enjoy." Says Nat.

"I'm sayin', love, I know you don't expect us to take you to a place you already got the directions to," Says Del.

"That'd be like ya'll livin' off our wealth and I know ya'll don't get down like that."

"No doubt, I know ya'll know the next level is about love and setting a foundation and building a strong family. Kids, wife, husband and a house." Says Ted.

"And preparin' for the future don't include bouncin' to VA. and splurgin'."

"True, say no more M-" says Nat then she moves in close to me, so close the shit makes me uncomfortable 'cause I haven't had another woman that close in years. Then the venom Queen whispers, "My directions lead right to you M and believe! When I get there, I'll be replacing whoever's there to permanently be in the passenger's seat right-" and she slowly runs her hand down my chest, "Next-" then down my stomach, "to"

Then around to my waist, "You M&M." Then they float away giving us the looks which have mentally destroyed ballas across the country and turned them into lames who now sit by the phone waiting for these Harlem venom Queens to call, praying they'll be blessed by these princesses. But their dreams will be just that, dreams of what could have been.

That night we drive back to Ted's crib to watch some flicks. It's like 7:00 and Ted says, "Why don't ya'll chill for awhile, we can get some cheesecake and ice cream. Von, you can get those new karate flicks you copped."

"He just got the NBA Live 2001 too." Says Eb.

"Oh good me and Eb can beat ya'll again for the championship," Says Gwen.

"We felt sorry for yall last time," says Ted.

"Yeah yeah whatever. We'll see," says Eb.

"Here, take my car cuzin'," Says Ted.

"Come on Eb, let's go with him," Says Gwen.

"OK just let me wash this park dust off my face," says Eb.

"I'll be downstairs,"

I bounce downstairs and stand at the car, not worrying about the women taking too long 'cause my man'll take care of that. Mentally I search the apartment for the movies when a voice interrupts my thoughts—.

Lights Out

For the first time in awhile, I'm not wakened by the sound of my son's mother cacklin' on the phone or yellin' at Tyriq for shit she can't yell at me about, and the shit's fuckin' with me. I lay quietly for a moment tryin' to sense the source of the evil shit that fills my realm— but I come up with nothing. I get my half and move to the bathroom to relieve myself. I rest on the edge of the bathtub inhaling deeply 'cause this peace and quiet is too ill, I feel like I'm on "The Cosby Show." I walk to the living room and . . . and . . . Yo what the fuck is all this shit?" The living room is filled with bags from the Gap, Footlocker, and all kinds of chicken-head stores and there— sitting on the couch— is my ghetto hoe, with her hair done and nails flossed and in the most expensive chicken head outfit I've ever seen. She smiles, somethin' I only see her do when she's torturin' us, and says "It's all for us, look—I got you some sneakers and a camcorder. I bought— "

"Tyriq." I bark and he says, "Yes daddy."

"Close your door . . . Where'd you get the doe for all this shit?"

"I got it from your stash."

"Are you fuckin' crazy? What the fuck you doin' goin' through my shit? I was usin' that money. I was flippin' it, but now shit is fucked 'cause yo stupid ass wants to be some soap opera bitch." She's silent because she's only seen me flip once before and that time she ended up with a swoll lip.

"Where's the rest of the money?"

"I spent it all I ain't know—if yo punk ass wouldnt've been hidin' shit, this wouldn't happen. Fuck you Red that's what ya bum ass gets for stashin' shit from me anyway. I don't know why the fuck you can't just-" Her words begin to melt together and becomes a loud irritating hum, like a message from the emergency broadcasting system. A rage I haven't felt in a long time begins to grow from the pit of my stomach as my plans to leave this living hell have been destroyed by the witch that is behind me, the one who disrespects me. The one who hates my son, the one who makes him cry himself to sleep at night, the one who only still lives because somewhere I once respected her position as the one who brought my son into this world, but that respect is gone. I turn arm extended and knock her against the living room wall; my hand wraps itself around her neck lifting her inches from the floor. As she gasps for air and claws at the force that suffocates her, a voice in my head tells me she's not worth killing. *You'll punish her more if you leave her in this crib all alone.* I release my grip of death and barely cover myself, pick up the necessary tools, and slide off.

I leave the building lookin' for refuge from the pain that I have come to know all too well, the only day I planned to get away from everything and just pack up and head for the hills, I get jammed. I can't get a fuckin' break, just when I tried to do some right, shit gets all fucked up. Fuck it, I'm gonna be here for the rest of my muthafuckin' life. Niggas wanna see me be a dweller, then I'll show them who the Red Silence really is.

*I end up at Myra's house, but she's not home which
sends me into an infuriating rage. I need her and she's not
around. Now I have to get revenge, someone gotta pay for
my grief. I steam across Riverside puffin' like a chimney and
searching my mind for a way out of this –from a distance I
peep some cat about to get in a 525 and I can smell the
money on him. I spot the jewels instantly, and he looks like
he's waiting for someone, probably his girl, they're gonna
have a little cool out night, the rain is on its way. But why
should he get to push a five and quarter? Why does he get
to have a nice girl and live love while I'm fucked up in the
game? Why THE FUCK SHOULD HE SHINE, I CAN'T—
FUCK THAT, IT'S STICK UP TIME. I desecrate the spirit
of the blunt and throw it to the ground with anger as if it
hasn't shown me nothin' but love over the years. I creep up
on money's stupid as. he doesn't even notice me I'ma get his
ass just for sleepin' and for thinkin' it can't happen, muthafucka'll probably fold when he sees the heat. "Give up the
cheese keys and jewels and keep your life."*

I've lived in New York long enough to have heard those
words before, and I know they're accompanied by a cold
steel object, which when discharged sends gun-powdered
propelled, sometimes hollow-tipped-cone-shaped monsters
into unprotected fleshy tissue. At one time, fear flooded my
body when a nigga flashed the heat, but it's been awhile
since I've heard those words, almost eight years, and it
doesn't affect on me like it used to. I just paid for this chain
and this ain't even my car. My man worked hard for his
ride. We earn our money, all the bullshit we have to go

through: credit checks, credit denials, refusals, office politics, and a hundred other things. And this nigga just comes along and takes whatever he wants 'cause he's too lazy or stupid to get his hustle on legally. Na, fuck that, I done had a gun pointed at me before and I'm still here, nigga gotta do better than that if he wants my shit.

Oh, this nigga thinks I'm playin' games. He must think it's somethin' sweet about me, nigga don't think I'm a killa-

My hesitation causes him to emphasize his seriousness with his ice grill, but the frozen face doesn't mean shit to me, it only works on niggas who ain't got one. Fuck this, plan time, I hand him the keys and as he reaches out I drop them—

Now he wanna be droppin'—OH shit! –muthafucka-

I grab the barrel and push it away from my body, and a shot explodes shattering the car window.

I should've clapped his ass when I had the fuckin' chance. This nigga's got some shit with him.

We struggle for the gun and the look in his eyes tells me he's surprised. Suddenly two more shots, the second knocks me against the car and I slide down still clutching the barrel of this death tool. This bitch nigga tried to rob me with no mask and now I got the mothafuckin' gun. I grab the gun by its handle ready to stop the nigga who tried to rob me and realize the trigger is crazy hard to pull. Somehow I gather enough strength to let off two shots, but . . .something's wrong . . .I can't . . . breathe. My chest . . . I'm shot oh God— oh . . . .I place my hand on the oozing red fluid that has been unwantingly removed from my body—blood—my blood . . . I'm gonna die cause I wouldn't give up the car. My momz is gonna be—black out—.

As the bullet knocks him down I see the pain in his face, I felt his pain. The nigga's strong, he never let go of the heat. He lifts the gun and lets off in my direction luckily he wasn't able to shoot.

Ebony walks down the slender hall of Ted's one bedroom headed for the living room when a sharp stabbing sensation causes her to stagger in pain, "Gwen something's wrong. Where's Von?"

"Ted just went to get him" says Gwen.

Downstairs blood leaks from my stomach and a raging fire blazes in my chest. Oh shit I'm shot . . . blackout. I come to not knowing how long I was out. Slowly I feel the air leave my body, and I feel like I wanna sleep, then the pain of something twisting my intestines revives me. I don't wanna die like this God, I'm too young. I didn't even do anything wrong, I've been living —Ted thanks God.

"Oh shit, yo, what the fuck. Damn sun— na shit, come on, not you kid," Says Ted. He kneels down next to me and, "Yo hold on nigga, it's gonna be alright."

"Yo the nigga tried to get me with no mask. Yo, don't let me die, I don't wanna die."

"You ain't gonna die nigga, not tonight. GWEN! GWEN!" Gwen and Ebony exit the building and screams of horror ring out through the street.

"Von-Von, no God no please, not my Von." Says Ebony. Tears flood their eyes as they kneel beside me.

"Call the ambulance, Gwen . . . Gwen." Says Ted. The horror that just filled my man's girl has her frozen, but she quickly comes to and dials. Ebony takes my hand and the gun falls to the floor and her fear and pain rush through my body reaching my soul trying to give me the strength to fight. Her attempt at calmness shows her strength, she knows she has to maintain for me to survive, I have to believe.

"Just hold on booby help is coming. You can't die on me yet, not now." Says Ebony.

I muster up enough energy to pull my shine from around my neck and, "Yo Cuzin if . . . I die— rock it with respect. And when my little brother is ready pass it on."

"Na fuck that nigga I'll hold it until you get out the hospital." Says Ted. Remarkably quick the ambulance arrives followed by a squad car and the attendants do their job. First the gurney then the mask,

"Where are you takin' him," says Ebony.

"Columbia Presbyterian." I pull the oxygen mask off and, "Go get my mother Eb."

"Von I'm not leavin' you." Says Eb.

"I'll get her don't worry." Says Ted. Just as my eyes begin to fail me again, I see Ebony's face which is filled with a petrifying fear. She thinks this will be the last time she sees me, but it won't be the last time she'll be threatened with the possibility of losing me.

I walk back to Myra's house this time letting myself in. I roll a godfather and blaze it. I can't believe I just hated a nigga whose worth was equal to my own. I, the Red Silence, hatin' a fellow renegade. Can I still call myself a professional? Am I worthy to keep the name I brandish? What the fuck I done did? The nigga looked down the barrel of the hamma and challenged it. Then after, he managed to survive the force of the subsonic he held onto the barrel like a champ and! He returned fire. A deep hurt fills my heart, not only for the renegade I violated but for all those who have been disrespected by ones who lost their status. For all those who hustle and were taken out 'cause they shined, this tear that runs from my eye is for those who can't knock the hustle. This godfather is for you, a nigga vows to make shit aiight.

As I unleash the sorrow of years past, Myra comes in and before she speaks a word she sits next to me and lays my head on her lap so she can look in my eyes when she says, "There's no pain here Popy, only love's in my house."

The next four days I spend with Myra, I never realized how happy she feels when I'm around her. She's helped to heal the grief that cuts through this ill ice heart. I sent the shorty across the hall to get the trees and the Dutches, and Myra always keeps extra clothes at her house for me so I ain't gotta leave for a minute. I lost the heat last night. I been to hell and back with that .45 and now it's gone, Myra said it was some kind of omen. Whatever it I,s it scared the shit out of me. Scared me so much I stayed in the crib for four days, and I ain't sleep right not one night.

I make moves to the roof to get some air. I ain't tryin' to be on the block just yet.

I lean on the ledge and watch the sun set over the East River giving way to the dark side. Again, I think about the last time I saw the sun. Really, I don't give a fuck no more. The shit is a waste of fuckin' time. I ain't never gonna get out of this melting pot of diseased life— I'm stuck here so I *might as well be the best I can be. Fuck it.*

As I enjoy the view, I'm total oblivious to the commotion created by New York's Fuckin' Finest. It seems they finally got up enough nerve to raid the block, and as they chase the renegades who won't give up without a fight, I'm caught up in the mix as I stand in the path of the famous getaway spot. Again I was off point and this is my punishment for breaking, not one, but four of the rules of being a professional. See you on the Island.

I come to feelin' like I was hit with a sledgehammer, and as I look around, I see my mother on the left, holding my hand asleep in those cheap blue cushioned chair/recliners. On my right is Ebony, asleep in a chair with her head on the bed. I try to sit up but I'm immobilized by an excruciating pain runnin' down my chest causing me to let out a muffled cry. It wakes my mother, "Ebony, he's awake, Ebony" she says. As she shakes her, they look at me and smile trying to hide the fear that lingers in their face. I can see through the masks. I try to speak but I feel like I've been swallowin' sand. Ebony grabs a cup as my mother gets a pitcher of water—both of them workin' to help the one they love. I guzzle the water and hold out the cup for the second round. I finish it off and in a dry hoarse voice say, "I should've just let him take what he wanted." My mother rubs my forehead, "It's not your fault. Just be happy you're still alive."

I can tell she's still in shock and stricken with grief. As they hold back the tears that begin to swell, there's a long silence—they're holding back somethin' their afraid to tell me, "I got shot in the stomach but my whole chest hurts." And the silence still lingers, Ebony's lip begins to quiver, "They had to . . .uh . . . cut you open and . . .look for the bullet." Again her tears fall like a summer's rain, "They said you'll be permanently scarred and you'll have some abdominal problems." It's hard to explain how minor that sounded at the time and how I couldn't understand why Ebony would be upset over a scar, I didn't want to upset her anymore so I tried to humor the situations, "Well, I guess I won't be workin' at no strip clubs." There's a slight lighting of the mood as they smile and giggle under their tears, it made me feel better. I change the subject, "Ma where's Sean and Devin?" They're my little brothers, Sean is 9 and Devin is 12, "I left them at you aunt's. They wanted to come, but I told them they had to wait until you were out of surgery." The anesthesia begins to send me back to my previous state, I try to fight it but it ain't workin'. Ebony can see I'm losing the battle and frees me from the urge to be courteous, "Von get some rest. We'll be here when you wake up." Just as I fade to black once again, she leans forward, and I can feel the warmth of her breath as she kisses me gently on my lips.

The next morning after hours of arguing, I send my two favorite women home, if not to sleep, then at least to shower and change clothes. Plus I need to get out this bed, and they're definitely not going to let me leave so they had to go.

Almost killing myself the first time, I tried to get up caused me to think of another way to get out of bed. I reach over and hit the remote and raise the head of the bed, and swinging my legs over the edge gives me freedom. I get up and search the closet for somethin' to cover my ass with 'cause this gown ain't makin' it. My Knick shorts are hangin' next to a sweat suit in the closet—once again they knew what I wanted before I did. Suited up and on the move, I drag myself and the I.V. stand to the bathroom. I can't bend over, so instead of lifting the seat, I pick a spot and fire. Just as the fluid moves through my body, a stabbing pain shoots through my stomach—uh, abdominal problems—more like abdominal destruction.

Walking lets me know how fuckin' painful this shit is, but it beats laying in the bed feeling sick and helpless. I walk past the nurse's station and two young nurses are conversin' on some real Jerry Springer shit, and from the shorter one's expression, it seems to be juicy. As I get closer, I can see her nametag, T. Simons resting on her breasts which are slightly exposed. The second button doesn't look like it's meant to be open. Her attention is drawn to the squeaking sound of the I.V. stand. The other nurse, interested in what changed her focus, turns and the smile on her face makes me nervous. She looks like a hungry wolf watchin' a plump sheep covered in A-1 steak sauce. "You know you shouldn't be up this early after surgery." the wolf says.

"Yeah, you have to give your body time to heal."

"Well I'm sayin', nobody told me so I'll just keep it movin'."

The wolf says, "You know we can force you to go back to your room if we have to."

"Don't think we won't take advantage of your weakened condition." Says Ms. T. Simmons And her face is sinister with a hint of sexual suggestion like she would love to take advantage of me. They both walk from behind the desk, and I try to change my direction swiftly like I had done days before on the football field, but of course it was impossible. I was snagged like a snake by a hawk. They escort me with much too delicate hands. Ms. T Simons' left hand is right on my lower back inside the gown, just a little too close for comfort. They return me to my depression chamber and my escorts try to make me comfortable. "If you need anything, anything at all, just buzz me." Yeah Ms. T. Simons would love for me to buzz her right here behind this curtain. "I'll be back later to give you a sponge bath." If I wasn't in love I would've welcomed a sponge bath by Ms. T. Simons but now- I gotta think of a way to protect my life, imagine if Eb walks in on my . . .I don't even wanna think about it.

Laying in this sickly position begins to fill me with frustration. Here I am at the prime of my life and on one of the best days of it—I get shot by some punk ass, stick-up kid. The nigga almost killed me and didn't get shit, if I ever . . .

I dwelled on my anger for what seemed to be hours when Ms. T. Simons interrupted my thoughts, "All right Mr. Davis, it's time for your sponge bath."

"Uh I'm sayin' I can walk around. I can just hop in the shower or tub. You don't have to-"

"No. You're not supposed to get those incisions wet, doctor's orders. So let me do what I do best. Don't worry I've done this plenty of times. I'll be gentle."

"I'm sayin', I can-"

"Relax, I'll take care of you." Just as Ms. T. Simons was about to rub me the too right way Ebony walks in, "Hey boo, how you feelin'?"

Ms. T. Simons says, "Miss. its time for his sponge bath. You'll have to wait outside until I'm done." Oh boy, she done fucked around and started some real shit. It's about to get hot. Ebony looks at Ms. T Simons name tag and, "Excuse me, uh Ms.—T—Simons, I know you just doin' your little job, but no one is going to sponge my man down against his will but me. Now I know I'm not as skilled as you may be in your itty-bitty white uniform, but I'm sure I can manage to stay away from the incisions." There's a moment of silence as if Ms. T. Simons was debating on whether to challenge her or not, but it's clear she ain't want none of Eb 'cause she folded like Crazy Eddie. "Fine, make sure the bandages don't get wet." And she hits her with the head-to-toe eye roll. "I will, and thank you—Ms.—T—Simons." The cleavage Queen leaves in defeat and Ebony says, "I—know—you—were not going to let her—"

"Don't even play ya'self."

"Yeah, you better not have." She kisses me while stroking my head and the look of relief has replaced the fear. "I thought I was goin' to lose you Von. You scared the shit out of me lying on the ground covered in blood-" her eyes slowly fill with tears as she relives her fear that night but she holds back, "I spoke to Ted, him and Gwen said they're comin' to visit around 7. I called your boss too. He said take off as long as you need. He said the contracts for Def

Jam have been finalized, and when you get a chance, send him the disk and dats so they can get started and he said he'll cover for you until you get back. You'll still get paid for the sessions. The check from the last two cleared, and your percent is in the mail. Your mother's bringing Sean and Devin by today and . . . what else . . . Oh, I put the Ac in the lot on 7th Ave. When I go back to work I'll get it out."

"What would I do with out you Eb? I hope I never have to find out."

"Don't worry Boo. You won't."

"I love you."

"You better. You smell like a sick old man, Boo. You need this bath."

My mother arrives after lunch with Sean and Devin who are more interested in seeing the incision then my well being. Sean is the youngest and most sensitive of us all. Seeing me like this seems to have changed his perception of life. I was always the almighty indestructible brother who could do anything and beat everyone, and now, here I am on what he may believe is my deathbed. His eyes say he's twisted by the idea of a force that could knock down his brother. This situation may be what causes him to be faced with the reality and power of life. Devin, on the other hand, sees this as giving me greater status. I survived a shooting, now I'm indestructible. I'm afraid that because he wants more than anything to be like me, and feels he is a younger version of me, maybe he'll try to follow in my footsteps and tempt death thinking he can win.

Ted and Gwen come through as the terror twins get on

my mother's last nerves, leading to a quick departure and a promise to return alone.

"What's the deal cuzin'? What you thought you was a super nigga?" Ted's big heart and bigger smile fill the dreary room with a lovable life.

"Hey Von, how you feelin'?" asks Gwen. I smile and shrug as she gives me her sorrowful face, "You scared Ebony half to death. We all thought you were done off." Gwen's tenderness and queen-like beauty make it easy to see why Ted wants to marry her. She's the only woman who even comes close to Ebony, "My Teddy bear was so worried about you, he stayed up all night waitin' for some word about you." Just then I realize how close Ted and I are. I know I would've felt the same way in this situation, but you never really understand how something will affect you until it happens.

"Yo Cuzin' you think you remember money?" asks Ted.

"No doubt. The nigga ain't even have on a mask. And he didn't take anything." Ted sticks his hand in his pocket and pulls out the chain and piece, "I told you I was only holdin' it till you got out. But since you aiight, you can take it back."

"Give it to Ebony, my chest is gonna be sore for awhile."

"I'm sayin', you know I got a license. We can bounce to Va and pick somethin' up. Drea from *Levels* is a D.T, so he can get you a vest."

My anger wants to take Ted's offer, but Ebony grabs my hand and I see the same fear in her eyes I saw the night before. She ain't really been around real violence, but as a young black man growing up in the midst of the crack war and being labeled public enemy #1 by the almighty

N.Y.P.D., along with every other black man between 13-25, I was forced to side with ones who fought for their lives. I was lucky enough to make it out alive and hide behind a job like Ted did, but when the time calls for us to defend our lives and the lives of the people we love, we return to our combat days in the trenches.

I look at Ted and he can read my answer and, "I'll let you think about it." To send the smokescreen and ease the minds of the two women who dread the day we have to return to the battlefields. He lightens the mood changing the subject to, "I saw Deny-Mo this morning. He came by the store and dropped off the tickets for the anniversary party. It's in three weeks. You should be able to go right?"

"No question, no way I'm tryin' to miss that. I ain't missed one yet and I ain't startin' now. We'll take my car, Eb can drive this time."

"Who said she wanted to drive?" says Gwen.

"He did." Says Ted.

Eb, "He ain't nobody." The bond that we've created has become stronger. Almost losing someone and almost being lost has made us appreciate and understand how precious life is. Ted and Gwen stayed until visiting hours were over, but Ebony had no intentions of goin' home. She brought an overnight bag so she wouldn't have to.

The next morning, I got a visit from an Officer DeCapo of the 23rd precinct. He asked me what happened, and listened, asked few questions and wrote everything down. He told me he was going to check the prints on the gun with my own and see if they could get a set of the prints on the gun.

I asked if I had to go to the station for that, and he said they already had them. They took them when I was under anesthesia. It was standard procedure. I don't think it is standard procedure. I think it was a niggacedure." My past experiences with police have taught me many things, but the last few years I managed to avoid being harassed by them and I forgot a few of the rules. 1) I didn't see anything, 2) I don't know nothin' and 3) if you say too much, you'll be a suspect. I forgot rule number three, a mistake I'll soon regret.

Nowhere to Hide

Five days later I'm released from the hospital and Ebony picks me up, "I forgot to tell you I made some changes around the house to brighten it up a little. "Changes, brighten it up. Or signals to let niggas know a woman's living there. Soon as we step inside, I check the bathroom status, the shower curtain and rugs are not black but her favorite color, and the blinds are now that burgundy again. Now I gotta survey all the damages. My sun blocking blinds are gone and replaced with thin curtains making it too bright that I ain't havin'. She also bogarded one of my closets and added some of her furniture. Damn I ain't been gone that long—and she was at the hospital everyday—so how—my mother, I almost forgot they're working together now.

"That detective called; he wants you to come down to the station." Says Eb.

"What! Hell no."

"Why not?"

"Rule number 4 in the Black man's guide to stayin' alive. Only go to the police station if handcuffed and dragged in against your will."

"Von—"

"Don't even start Eb. In N.Y., niggas have a strange way of endin' up dead in police stations."

"But you didn't do anything wrong; he just wants to help."

"Help who? How many dead niggas ain't do nothin'. Them muthafuckas ain't gonna do nothin' but help me to an ass whippin' or a jail cell. In the eyes of the almighty N.Y.P.D., every nigga is guilty of somethin', and they just haven't caught him doin' it yet. Believe if they want me to be guilty of somethin', they'll find a way to make it happen, and there won't be a damn thing anybody can do about it."

"But don't you wanna find the guy who shot you?"

"Listen Boo, New York ain't as big as niggas think, and believe one day I'll bump into him again. And this time, it'll be a day when I'm with one of those crazy niggas I don't hang around with too much 'cause they are beef. They'll be glad to give me New York justice. And who said the police give a fuck enough to stop shootin' niggas 40-50 times to look for him.

Two days later, I was arrested for gun possession and attempted murder—see my fingerprints were all over the gun and I had gunpowder on my fingers. I also told them I let off one shot at money and that was a confession of attempted murder. I was booked and released on $25,000 bond. I've waited for this day since I was 15 and because I allowed my defenses to slip, I've been captured by the enemy. Now I must prepare myself for the battle I'll have to fight in their territory. I'll have to become something in order to survive in this war. I don't know what or who I'll have to become, but it scares the shit out of me. I know what I had to do in order to make it through that crack shit and I didn't like it. Every nigga I know that went to war comes out fucked up and poisoned forever. Niggas that came out of epidemics with Purple Hearts don't go to jail and become victims. I don't know what I did to deserve this but . . . like my mother always told me: "Do what you gotta do to stay alive."

The court proceedings were quick and painful. My lawyer got them to drop the attempted murder as long as I pled guilty to the gun charges—sentence no less than 2 Ω years and no more than 6 in a state correctional facility. If I would have went to trial I think I would of blown. My mother wanted to fight it if I believed in my lawyer, so did Eb—but I ain't have enough money to get the Johnnie C team. And the way I see it he's the only nigga who can get a Black man off when the shit's this thick. And my lawyer was white, and I know this don't sound politically correct or very intelligent, but he's white and I can't see myself having faith in a muthafucka who'll go have drinks with the same muthafucka who's tryin' to take my freedom. So I took the best of the worst. I was literally dragged out the courtroom because my anger took over when I saw my mother's face filled with a deep ancient pain. Imagine the first African woman brought to America on the slave ship. Now picture the anguish in her face when her child was sold and taken from her and you'll understand a part of my rage.

That night I was taken to Rikers Island, the largest county jail in America; I was taken to C-74 mod 5 main, the 4 buildin', the adolescent buildin' affectionately called the "animilescent" buildin'. Fuck—yo I was just convicted for tryin' to stop a nigga from robbin' me. And now I'm in fuckin' jail, 'cause of another muthafucka. But on the real, I knew this shit was gonna happen I hid from the enemy for a long time, and they finally snagged my ass. You can run but you can't hide. I'm escorted through the hallway at 3 a.m., and I'm numb. The corridors are a half mile long, with a number of housing modules. It's like walkin' through the halls of hell on my way to my eternal damnation. There's an eerie silence like there's no life, no warmth, no souls. I'm going to die here and no one will ever know. Even though it's only a half hour away from the city, I still feel like I'm a million miles from home.

The night officer in 5 main is Will, my man Mike's little brother. Both of them been comin' to *Levels* as long as I have. "I heard you was getting sentenced today, and I knew you'd be comin' through, so I got this shift so I could hip you to the game. Aiight, forget about everything you know about the outside world because none of that shit applies here. First thing, there's two phones: one for Black one for Spanish, if you get caught usin' the wrong one you'll end up in the infirmary. There's five cats who got the Black phone locked down from 8:00 to click. If you use it durin' their time without their permission you'll end up cut up. Don't be in the TV room too much—a lot of shit goes on because of it. Take a shower with your drawers on and watch your back, niggas get stabbed in there.

Here, carry one of these whenever you leave the unit— to the infirmary, the gym, the yard, or to the visit, just don't take it on the floor." He hands me a razor blade and a tooth-brush with two razors on either side of it on the outside of the bristles. "And if someone tells you let's take it to the shower or a riot breaks out use this, sleep with it under your pillow with one eye open. The third weapon he gives me is a thick piece of slender steel rod sharpened to a point with a sheet taped around the bottom for a handle. The blade is at least six inch long. "If there's a shakedown I'll let you know so you can stash the bangers. Yo kid shit is crazy as hell on the Island. Don't trust anyone and always set it first. If you're quiet and stay low you might make it out aiight. I won't be able to help you if some shit jumps off so you're all alone. One more thing, all the niggas at the shop said they'll look out for your girl, and we'll keep the slimy niggas away from her. Hold ya head nigga 'cause it's about to get thick."

The Dark Knight Lives

Ah, a very familiar scene, C-73, the 3 buildin' on the Island. I been up north a few times, and I been to almost every county jail on the East coast, but the Island is the worst place of all. Imagine every criminal in the five bor-oughs placed on one island. How can anyone control all them crazy muthafuckas with psychopathic tendencies? I'll be callin' this home for a minute.

There's 60 of us in the holdin' pens waitin' to be housed in a unit. A lot of niggas is comin' up out their shines 'cause the predators got the prey thinkin' all kinds of shit. "Yo kid, come up out of that, you don't wanna go up in there and get blasted for yo shit." Or "Yo kid, take this 20 dollars for that ring. You can buy you some cigarettes or somethin'. You're gonna need it." If a muthafucka goes for some lame-ass shit like that then he deserves to get jacked. Fear is the first sign of being easy pray, if niggas find out you can be got they'll all swarm down on you like locusts. We're now officially in the belly of the beast and a nigga gotta be ready for anything 'cause niggas in here love the smell of blood. If a muthafucka smells the slightest bit of weakness in you, he's comin' for whatever he can get, material or not. A muthafucka might just wanna assert his fuckin' authority and use you to prove to other niggas that he's got power. On the low, . . . I love this shit—it scares the hell out of me.

I been in holdin' for hours. It's been awhile since I been through bullpen therapy. Then the C.O says, "Wilson—8 main—house of pain baby." Last time I was here, 8 main was the illest dorm in the buildin'. They called it the house of pain cause if you weren't a live wire, niggas would keep you around just to use you for shit. Many times I watched niggas washin' five or six nigga's drawers. A grown ass fuckin' man washin' another niggas drawers! What kinda shit is that? How fuckin' scared could you be? Luckily I'm well prepared. While I was waitin', I pulled out the rug cutters from my sneaker and placed them in my mouth, between my cheek and teeth. That's the quickest way to pull my gats—on the real, it's like an Island tradition. With my joints in my mouth, I can just blow and my shit magically appears and lets loose on some clown nigga.

The walk to 8 main brings back memories, and slowly I slip into a bloody state of mind—that's the only way I'll be able to survive. I reach the vestibule of 8 main and the tension is on, fake thug niggas is watchin' like I'm one of the new niggas comin' through—they hopin' to find a vic.

This unit's got four tiers on each side and 15 cells on each.

Each one of my new neighbors is sizin' me up. They want my chain. My camouflaged steelo got niggas thinkin' I can't make it happen, I like that—I wanna nigga to test me—I miss the beef. I miss the blood soaked gat I hold in my mouth. I miss takin' a niggas heart with one slice—yeah 8 main house of pain. It's about to be on.

The C.O. in the bubble cracks the A side, and I slide in on some mask of The Red Death shit. I'm blessed with the cell at the end of the tie. Good, I need to watch niggas. The two razors in my mouth 'cause me to smile to myself cause these muthafuckas don't know they're in for a bloody treat. The cell door slams close behind me, and I don't even bother to unpack my bundle or make my bed. I might not be here too long, I got a feelin' I'm gonna have to rub my gat across a nigga's eyes. Remember when I said I had that remembrance curse? Well to help my memory, I've learned to make all my razor incisions unique so I know who I had beef with. Most of these niggas I'll end up bumpin' heads with up

north, and I can't have some bandit creepin' on me or set-
tin' me up for some old shit I did. I come through just before
the midday count, and while I'm waitin' for it to clear, I
search my cell for weapons. A nigga might've left something
because he had to travel light or went home. I check the
usual hiding places: the mattress, the locker, bed frame,
radiator—jackpot! Aww shit! Happy birthday to me. Yeah,
this shit gotta be at least six inches. This is a nice one too—
standard Plexiglas molded into the shape of a dagger with
a rag for the grip. I sit on the bed inspecting my weapon
schemin' on how I'll get it bloody—a heist—the phone. The
phones are the cause of 80% of the beef on the Island the
other 20% is about money, disrespect, and drugs. The
phones are used according to how much dough you got in
your account. If you don't have any, you still get 15 minutes
free. If you can get a nigga's state I.D. numbe,r you can
make a call. The more numbers you have the longer you can
rock. A lot of weak niggas give up their numbers so nobody
don't fuck with them, so imagine how much drama can go
on when predators and prey live under these conditions. All
the things that are a connection to the outside world are a
desired commodity. Whoever controls these connections has
power, in here power and the perception of it is everything.
There's plenty of predators on the Island which makes gain-
ing power a challenge. Then there's bootleg predator nig-
gas who front like they got heart but are really just makin'
moves. I'm an official predator so I ain't worried 'cause I
know all the punk muthafuckas'll bow down to who ever
takes charge of the phone time. Oh yeah, there's one cat or

clique who runs the phone and they monitor all calls, who can call and at what time and for how long. Fuck that, I ain't a vic.

On the lockout, I slide in the day room, which is a large room about half the size of a high school gym, I need to peep the structure of my new environment. I roll through and pass the Halle Berry look alike in a C.O.'s uniform, and she hits me with a full body check and I ignore her 'cause I know she wants me to sweat her. I slide a chair to the back of the room, frontin' like the T.V.'s got my attention. The T.V. sits in the center of the room against the far wall, and there's large Playskool plastic tables and chairs scattered around. I sweep the room discreetly to see who's frontin', and who's on some just to get rep shit, and most important who's runnin' the phone. But most of all, can the muthafuc-ka really hold it down?

The rest of the day I spend in silence, waiting patiently. Then I decide to try the bitch ass muthafucka and his punk ass faculty who's claim to be runnin' the jack. The phones go off at 11:00 and this bitch nigga's come up to me for the fifth time since I been here. He wants to know if I wanna use the phone. Of course I do, but I ain't tryin' to get the little punk-ass 15 minutes he's tryin' to give me.

The phones are against a wall in the day room. There's a table and chair in front of it so niggas can chill. A fake cool out spot.

It's now 9:30. I go to the jack with my jacket and pillow. The pillow hides the ox I found in my cell, and the jacket is in case niggas try to cut me. I lean on the table with the—

ox ready and gats in mouth, I dial Kenya, "Hello."

"Yo it's Red."

"What's up?"

"Yo, I'm on the Island love. Tell Storm I'ma send him a shorty so she can bring me some scommas like three times a week."

"How much you need?"

"Like a quarter."

"What else?"

"I'll probably be down like three joints—so keep that little nigga alive and on the streets, Kenya. I'ma need him when I get home."

"I think Nonye's gonna keep him."

"Word?"

"Yeah, I can see it, she's feelin' the nigga."

"Cool, just make sure he don't get caught up."

"Aiight, yo Red."

"Yeah?"

"Come back to us nigga."

"I'll try. One."

"Love." Kenya always took care of a nigga. Whatever I needed, she gave, not money wise but when shit got a little thick in the game, she was there, especially when I needed to be without the heat.

Fifteen minutes go by and I dial again—this time one of the corner pay phones in front of Drew Ham projects. The local chickens are always outside, and if Red asks they shall deliver. As the phone rings, the fake-ass regulator tells me my time is up—I ignore the command. "Yo this Red who dis?"

"Hi Red, this Niecy."

"What's goin' on love?"

"Nothin'. "Time to set up the game on shorty, "Yo Toya out there?" I know she's not.

"No."

"Damn!"

"Why, what's wrong?"

"I'm on the Island and she was supposed to be pickin' up something and bringin' it to me." The phone falls silent as she thinks about cuttin' Toya's throat.

"I'm sayin, if you want . . . I'll bring it."

"I'm sayin' I don't want you to get in any trouble."

"It's OK Red, I wanna see you anyway."

"Word. Why?"

"I'm sayin', you know I been diggin' you since I was a shorty and you was getting money on my block."

"So why you ain't never check me?"

"'Cause you was the fly nigga on the block and I thought you wouldn't be tryin' to see me like that."

"See you ain't never say nothin' so I never knew." This dumb little bitch don't know she about to be my new trooper.

"So if I did—what—you would have been tryin' to get at me?"

"Come check me and we'll talk about it. Aiight?"

"Yeah."

"Aiight, now listen, go to Shaka Zulu's and tell him you need to see Storm and he'll bless you."

"O.K."

"Yo Niecy-"

"Huh?"

"I should've got with you instead of Toya."

"I'll see you soon aiiight?"

"Aiight." Niecy's only 17 and open on the fact that a superstar like me is interested in her. Even though she hung up, I stay on the jack—I want the shit to thicken.

Slowly my heart begins to race as the second phone check comes. It's been awhile since I felt like this. It's like the rush I got when I was on the run from these Cuban cats. I got 'em for four bricks of fish scale. These niggas was so large, niggas wouldn't even buy it off me. I couldn't give the shit away. The niggas put a hit out on me and I ran for like two months. I never knew when a nigga was gonna push my wig back, but it was a ill thrill—non stop action—life on the line bullets flyin' I loved every minute of it. And now—the rush has returned.

A half-hour goes by, now I'm surrounded by niggas mumblin' shit, it sounds like threats but I can't hear it so **FUCK'EM**. Again, the phone check comes, "Hold on, I'll be just a minute." I say. Now I'm testin' niggas and my heart's racin' cause I know it's about to be on. An hour goes by—both my hands is crampin' up and getting sweaty cause I'm holdin' the ox crazy tight. The adrenaline is rushin' through my body making me tremble, at first I think it's fear, and . . . no not fear . . . excitement! I'm crazy charged! I'm tremblin' with anticipation of the bloody carnage that's about to happen. I know these niggas won't be able to take it much longer—I'm straight up shittin' on these niggas, blatant disrespect—-the shit I'm doin' is about to get me *murdered. I love it, the cowboy has returned.*

11:00—lock in—now I'm fuckin' mad. Nobody did shit, punk muthafuckas. Niggas is all walkin' back to their cells talkin' mad shit like I give a fuck after I just took their hearts. I pick up the phone receiver, disconnect the wire, and carry it back to my cell. See this is just what I'm talkin' about, nigga's frontin' like he's a live wire. He was probably running with some niggas who left him the phone, and all he had to do was build a clique around it. Livin' off another nigga's shine. And! His clique is crazy butt 'cause if they was "bout it" one of them would've jumped with no question

I slept well after settin' up a new schedule for the house. The next morning, I'm up early—gat in hand just in case, but I ain't too worried about these niggas. The fake-ass jack regulator is the first nigga I step to. I ask the nigga if he had a problem with the way I was layin' shit down and if so, "Let's take it to the showers and go gun-to-gun." He fell back with no resistance. "Yo I'm takin' 2:30 to 3:00 and 9:30 to 11, the rest you niggas it pass around accordin' to your hand." Yeah my shit falls into place.

The Eclipse

The unit is a large 40-bed room. The beds are lined up 20 on one side, 20 on the other with small waist-high steel lockers next to each one. The day room is next to the front steel door and the showers are off to the left near the officer's control room. That room is surrounded in Plexiglas which allows the corrections officer to see the whole room clearly. The Plexiglas window in the day room and the C.O.'s bubble are covered with the black iron gate.

The first few days I just followed the routine 'cause the shock still had me twisted. After I get my first visit from my momz and Eb, I started to feel a little better then . . . the demons smell a victim.

The Island has a commissary where you can buy toiletries, cakes, and soda and a small variety of snacks. (Like giving a bunch of criminals large amounts of sugar will help subdue them.)

The dorm has just come back from commissary and as I sit on the bed after securing my stash, I get that feelin' you get when someone's watchin' you. I brush it off and reach for the *Source* Magazine Ebony brought me. Then the feeling hits me again like a slab of concrete. I look around and see two Spanish cats sizin' me up from the other side of the dorm. My heart begins to beat a little faster as it realizes somethin' is about to jump off. Call it my New York intuition. I open my locker blocking their view of my intentions and remove the toothbrush razor from its hidin' place, then I grab a bag a chips to camouflage the action. I avoid eye contact as blood rushes through my veins, causing a sensation of heat to fill my body. My palms become sweaty as I try to adjust my weapon in my hand under the protection of the magazine. I try to plan my defense but . . . aw shit, here they come. Oh shit, oh shit, oh shit . . .nowhere to run to, the C.O,. in the bubble ain't –fuck that. Come on nigga, you ain't no punk, these muthafuckas is unarmed just stay calm and shit won't get messy. OK. OK. Stay calm,

stay—"Ayo money, my man and me was wonderin' if you
would just give up your commissary without a fight 'cause I
really don't feel like cuttin' a nigga today?" Now what—if
you give up your shit, they'll come back every day, then
they'll want more. Then they won't let a nigga have shit.
They'll be doggin' you every day or I can cut one and pray
to God the other one . . . No time for weighing it, you know
what you gotta do.

The next bunk is like 3 feet away from me, and they're
both standin' in front of it. I jump up tackling the one closest to me while simultaneously glidin' the toothbrush down
the front of the second one's face. Purely out of instinct I
went for the face. Behind me I hear him scream as his man
and I played peek-a-boo with my razor and his hands and
face. Within seconds, I leap to my feet in fear that number
two would attack from behind, and just as I rise, he removes
his hands from his face causing my weapon of destruction to
create a puzzle of his features to give the doctors a challenge
when putting him back together again. The first one gets up
off the bed and reaches for . . . I don't know what! But fear
causes me to shred that hand and arm with no mercy.

I back away from the scene that I would later realize
made me cross the line between prisoner and inmate.
Someone taps me from behind, "Yo Sun, take off your shirt.
You got crazy blood on you." I respond with no hesitation,
using the blood splattered clothes to clean my hands and
weapon. The voice handed me a replacement and, "Gimme
the gat." I clutch it still like a warrior never wanting to let
go of his weapon in the heat of battle. "Come on nigga, I'm

gonna stash it, now give it up." I let it loose knowing I have another if I need. Next thing I know I'm in the day room watching Caliente and some nigga's whisperin' Johnnie C style in my ear, "Just chill Black. Be easy." I look to my left and the tank top wearin', dark skinned baldhead cat gives me a head nod to OK my position. I had just become a victim of circumstance. Yet I made a power move without even knowing. See, these niggas next to me run the jack and I just took two phone times in one scene now I'm two steps ahead of the game.

Days pass and Halle Berry's now showin' signs of tacky hoe status. She thinks I'm not recognizin' her shine. This shit can be a touchy situation 'cause she can cause a lot of unnecessary shit to jump off. I really ain't got no time to entertain her bullshit, but if I don't' she'll act the fuck up. Yeah, I'ma have to give her a little airplay now and then, just to keep my business right.

There's four major gangs on the Island: the Bloods, Latin Kings, Nietas and Muslims. Then you got the renegade niggas, like me, the niggas who don't' give a fuck about the gangs, and then you got the cats who just tryin' to live. In this dorm, there's 19 Nietas, one King and the rest are civilians and renegades. Of course, it's hard for them to accept that I'm runnin' one of the jacks so the tension stays thick, but niggas ain't got no heart so nobody's jumped yet. It's only a matter of time before somebody will want to force my hand, or a nigga who ain't got the heart to step to me will talk some other clown nigga into doin' it. I think I'll make an example out of a nigga to prevent shit, but right now ain't nobody ready to jump. Fuck it—it's the Rock, somethin' will pop off soon.

Life in the house of pain continues to run smooth and I make Halle's job easier. I keep the house quiet, not silent but not rowdy. The fights are kept to a minimum and niggas just stay in check. I just gotta make sure I don't allow myself to suck up to her and play her close like all these other niggas. Imagine being surrounded by niggas all day and being one of the only chics they see 24 hours a day. No question the attention is off the meter, and it most likely will distort your perception. Then one day a nigga comes along who acts like you don't exists and he ain't gay. If you're not secure with yourself, you might start to act stupid and do dumb shit to be noticed. Example, one mornin' on the lock-out, she conveniently forgot to open my cell, and didn't open it until she was good and ready, like she had more important shit to do. Then another time, a nigga was on the jack and she stood like 2 feet away from me talkin' crazy loud to the relief offi-cer, so loud I couldn't hear my peoples on the other end. I definitely gotta watch her ass.

"Wilson 28 cell on the VI." Yeah, no doubt, a night visit, Niecy's provin' to be a real trooper. She ain't miss a visit yet. I bounce to my cell and grease up well so I can cheek these balloons she's bringin'. Swiftly I'm buzzed out and on my way.

At the VI entrance, I change into the jumper and meet my little shorty for the scomma swap and a nice feel up or a heavy dose of finger to coochie stimuli. Yeah, Niecy don't play no games. She gets down for everything. There's like 80 niggas in here and they all got anywhere from one to three people with them. That's like 160-200 people, and believe I can touch and feel and nut off if I play it right.

An hour later I'm nicely packed, coochie hand well scented and entering the dorm ready to spark up. I lay in the cut and roll the Dutch I copped from the night officer. It's almost 9:00 p.m and the fake jack regulator let's me know it's free, but tonight, a nigga feels like forcin' his hand—just to see how much power I got. Now I ain't know the fake Halle was catchin' feelings today 'cause I ain't been in the same room with her since the wake up and now she's feelin' even more neglected 'cause now I'm stayin' in my cell. Sometimes we do casual convo but not nothin' too real cause she got too much pride to roll her bootleg ass down to my cell. Which means if she's in a bad mood today, some shit is about to jump off—how and when will be up to me. Why—'cause I'm jumpin' out the pan and into the fire tonight.

I get the second shout-out for the jack and I let it hang, I'm smokin' an L—I don't feel like being bothered—all of a sudden I hear Halle yellin' 'cause sound carries in this buildin' and I can hear everything. She's flippin' in the rec room talkin' 'bout how everybody in here is a punk bitch for lettin' me run the phone, only cowards would let a tall skinny kid like me run shit. Now it's—10:00. I'm really pushin' my authority to the limit—this bitch is tryin' to get the whole house to flip on me, and I'm not stoppin' it. I need some beef.

Out of habit, I pace in my cell plannin' for the possible

outcome—*if a nigga goes against the grain and picks up the jack, I'ma have to air his ass out. If it's a Spanish cat, not only will I get moved out the house and lose the phone, but I'll have beef with the whole buildin' 'cause right now they got the 3 buildin' locked down.*

I wait quietly blazin' another blunt, anticipatin' the outcome, listening carefully to the emotions exploding from the bootleg chic's mouth. Then . . . nothin' . . . fear lasts longer than love. But you never know she might've gave some nigga a little more heart.

The next mornin' the day officer calls yard, and as always I don't' go. It's a no win situation for me. All the leaders of the Spanish gangs in this buildin' hold court. Each house is supposed to have a lieutenant who speaks for that house. On several occasions, niggas done gave orders to hit me up, but the shit never jumped off 'cause muthafuckas never had the courage to do it. If there's a hit out and a nigga doesn't do his job, that soldier is then hit up for disobeying. So if out of nowhere a cat gets cut, then disappears from my house, it means he didn't do his job.

Most of the time when yard comes back, I watch these niggas just to get a vibe—today I got a feelin' I should study the body language of my enemies. I watch in suspense wonderin' whose tension is near its peak, and who'll have the heart to step to me. Niggas know they gotta kill me for the jack, and if they don't, I'll kill them and they ain't ready to play that game. I got a feelin' niggas is getting antsy, and it's time to lay down my law with surgical skill. A nigga's gotta keep order; niggas might feel like they can test me. I

can't take the chance of these Spanish cats jumpin' me. Time
to make a German bleed—why—'cause to me—paranoia is
a finer scale of reality.

The next days I spend being schooled on the politics of
jail by the cat that looked out for me after my first display of
carnage. His name is Brook, a typical Brooklyn gunslinger—
22 and locked up for pullin' a string of robberies in Jersey.
The D.A. had evidence on only one and Brook always said,
"They only got me on one of many." He was one of those cats
who seemed as regular as the nigga you went to high school
with, intelligent, attentive, yet extremely dangerous. One
thing I don't like about him is he's too unpredictable. You
never know when he's gonna flip. One minute he'd be talkin'
calm with you or laughing and somebody might say somethin' that pisses him off and he'll whyle out with no warnin'.
He never flipped on me but I always feel like if I said the
wrong thing he would. Yet he never said he would, matter of
fact, he always seemed to try to hold me down, but I still got
a problem trustin' the nigga.

Because of my skill to display bloody scenes, I was
allowed peak jack hours, the Spanish cats had 8 to 8:45 and
now I did, and with this new privilege came a few other
perks. I also had a clique to look out for me and watch my
back if anything got hectic. I didn't have to worry about niggas tryin' to extort me or make me pay rent. A nigga could
live in peace—or so I thought.

One day Brook, Lance, and me were in the day room as
always, watchin' videos, one of our only connections to the

outside world. Lance slid off and came back with a blunt. I smoked weed briefly after high school, but quickly grew out of it. I couldn't get anything done being off in another world. But right now, I'll do anything that'll help me dull my senses and cure the pain that fills the very depths of my being.

I drag lightly because I'm fairly new to this herbal scene, yet I know how notto choke on the thick cloud of green buds. Three and pass that's the rule, by the third round, my field of vision narrows and the weed demon takes control. My mind becomes fuzzy and the fire of the inner hell that destroys my soul temporarily cools. The pain is gone . . . for the moment. I have found my escape . . . thank you God . . . not God . . . he would never . . . a spirit. The spirit of destruction that controls this world of dread and malice.

A week later I'm takin' blunts to the face—dolo. And I've become one of them, fearless and ruthless. The herbal tranquilizer found a way to transform my pain into anger and finally . . . *RAGE*.

$ $ $ $ $ $ $ $

On one of my weed induced days, two Kings come into the unit, word is they lookin' for the moreno who blazed their two brothers. I waste no time. I gotta release this raging ball of fury that has built up inside of me. Feelings other than anger, malice, manipulation, and hate are considered a weakness and a nigga that shows less than the rule is and will be prey to the predators.

The two unsuspecting victims make up their bunks as I

approach with the dual razored tipped object that has become one with my hand. I stand in slicin' range with my hand slightly behind my leg, "What's up fellas? Yo, I heard you was lookin'

for the cat who blasted your brothers."

"Yeah, why you know him?"

"Something like that." And with blindin' speed I sent my razored friend sailing across the cheek of the tattooed one. His brother charges and me, lowering his shoulder hitting me right in my chest. I slide across the linoleum floor and jump to my feet as if unaffected by the blow. He blows into his hand and a razor appears between his fingers. He comes in range and I reach out and offer to introduce him to my friend he declines and introduces me to his. My wrist stings as blood slowly rises to the surface. I attack from a different angle, this time comin' from below, and once again, his razor met with my skin partin' it like a ripe banana. Just then two C.O.'s enter the dorm area. One is like 6'1" and three times my size. The next one is equal except a few inches shorter. The tallest stands at a distance and, "Aiight fellas, that's enough. I don't wanna have to pull the pin on you niggas. Now drop the bangers and let's hit the infirmary." On the Island, you don't argue when you get a break from the C.O.'s., a situation like this one definitely calls for some bing time. When you act up in jail, they send you to jail for inmates. I ain't never been to the bing, but I heard it's fucked up, and I ain't tryin' to go so I chill.

After the infirmary, I was sent to another buildin' C-75 to prevent any more beef with the Kings.

The new unit got more black niggas than Spanish niggas, so I ain't got too much to worry about. The duty officer just happens to be the ex-wife of one of my mans from *Levels*. Good thing she wasn't mad at my man and hatin' on me. She told me my man, Drea made sure I got into her house. This nigga Lance I was in the four buildin' with got moved out a couple of days before I did. And some niggas from around his way got the shit on lock in here so niggas is showin' me love off the strength of Lance and my semi friendship with the cute-ass C.O. Yeah, I shouldn't have any beef in here.

The next couple of days run just as I want, but like always, two Latin Kings come in and force my mothafuckin' hand. Whenever more than two of them get together, there's trouble—fuckin' Germans. The one king that was in the house was happy with his time 'cause I let'em live on my jack. The Nietas is deep in here and money had to pay for phone time. Now his two fake-ass thug brothers come in and the muthafuckas got issues.

Holdin' down the jack takes a little more than the ability to instill fear in niggas. Every time some new niggas come in the house, I have to weigh and judge the scene. Should I blast him before he even thinks about the phone? Should I let him live, or should I make him a solider? One of the new Kings approaches my cell.

"Yo you run the phone?"

"Yeah."

"Yo, can you give me some time?"

"Nope."

"Yo, I'm sayin'—"

"No!"

"Damn, gimme some space."

"Yo, don't ask me no more!" See, I already know that if I give him time, I gotta give his man time—then these niggas is gonna get greedy and try to take over shit. So instead of waitin' for the heat, I bring it. The nigga comes back like 10 minutes later this time with his man and his hand in his pocket. He's talkin' real loud too; he wants slot time, yatta, yatta, yatta. I'm cool as a fan, emotionless, straight rock face, watchin' that hand in the pocket. I'm thinkin' I'll be able to spit out before he even thinks about pullin'.

Now the mothafuckas blowin' his cool—I still stay quiet, then the bullshit begins to bore me, I remove the small 6-inch sword from under the mattress and, "I'm sayin' money you wanna bleed for that slot time." He quickly pulls his hand out his pocket—full bluff mode, he never even had a gat.

Again, the days seem to melt together because of the routine, and it's like we're all in one big line waitin' our turn to go home. Some of us'll be on the streets in a couple of months others in years. It's like one long fuckin' day.

As time passes, the fake thug's animosity grows. Every time I turn around, my name is comin' out his fuckin' mouth, but I keep actin' like I don't know. I want it to build up so when I step to him, he'll blow, then I can blow.

Saturday afternoon, I play my regular post, day room window open feet on a table and a fan blowin' the smoke outside. The 6-inch sword is by my nuts. The razors are in my *mouth and like 20 niggas old enough to be my father are askin' me if they can use the phone—for 15 minutes of course. And the fake Ms. Berry calls her friends down on her lunch break to witness my cinematic debut, complete with techno-vision and Dolby surround. I lounge at the far end of the rec room and . . . Boooom! The tier door busts open and E.R.U. rushes in. They're ten deep and none of them is less than 6 feet and 200 plus. I grab my emergency empty milk carton, slide the baby sword in it, step on it, and kick in the middle of the floor. I get up squat down and stuff the balloons from my pocket, as they close in on the day room I spit out the razor and toss it behind the TV with the blunt. I scan the scene and mad niggas are in full stash mode. If niggas is dirty, they'll be catchin' a royal ass whippin'.*

The first victims get thrown against the wall, I check my pocket to make sure I 'm clean and—shit! A small baggy of weed—no time, niggas is pushin' me against the wall. The baggy rests between the wall and my palm and stress has just taken over. Quickly a nigga brings an ultimate calmness to my cipher, and I think how I'm gonna play these E.R.U. niggas with skill. The C.O. finishes searching me and swift-ly I give rise to a new level of effortless skill by letting exe-cution unfold beyond technique and beyond exertion. I slide my arm wide alone the wall before allowing the baggy to slip from my hand just enough to scoop it from a different angle before it falls to the floor. Really—I'm the superior nigga in this get-over game 'cause nobody peeped shit. "All right, you muthfuckas know the drill nut to butt," shouts one of the C.O. They line us up, hands behind our heads and so

close if the nigga in front of me bent over with no warning
I'd unwillingly become a homo. They search the day room
and find a few unstashed bangers and my blunt but not the
razor. Then they yell somethin' about give up all the shit
now and, yatta, yatta, yatta, yatta. Right now I'm hot, I
could've went down for some real bullshit. Halle knows
she's supposed to tell us the squad is comin'-time to put her
ass in check.

After cell checks, the squad bounces and I head straight
to the bubble. Halle buzzes me in and says, "Listen love, it's
obvious you got a problem with my status, so let's handle
this now."

"What? What are—"

"Yeah whatever. Listen, from now on let me know when
the squad is comin' and stop tryin' to get these niggas to flip
on me 'cause it ain't gonna happen. You ain't given up no
sex, so they ain't tryin' to bleed."

"I know—"

"Yeah just make sure you let me know, and I'll give you
a little airplay on the low."

Then I breeze leavin' her stuck with nothing but passion.
She's just another victim of my thugs passion. Yeah she can't
knock the hustle.

I step in the day room and that big mouth King is talkin'
about me again. Time to test him. The whole house is watching TV so I cut if off hoping an audience will help Money
decide to jump. Every one waits for my speech as I step up
to Bluff Daddy's chair. "Listen, it seems you've got a problem with the way I'm runnin' the fuckin' jack. There'll be no

*jumpin' 'cause I know how ya'll get down like that. It'll be
me and you, gun to gun right now, and if you don't have one
I'll give you one."* I pull out the sword drop it on the floor
in front of him and, *"Now what!"* He just looks at it and
looks at me . . . nothing . . . bitch-ass nigga. I pick it up and,
"You lost your chance, now shut the fuck up." I told one of
my sons to turn the TV back on and I bounce—blunt time.

The following weekend Ebony comes to see me. The
visiting room is a wide open space with rows of plastic
chairs and knee-high tables. I put on the gray jumpsuit and
slippers, and scan the sea of heads that fill the . . . Ebony.
Her radiant glow lights all,

"What happened to your arm?!!"

"Nothin', I just had a little accident."

"What! What kind of accident?"

"It's nothin', I hurt myself playin' basketball."

"Von, you don't play ball good enough to have an accident."

"I'm sayin'-"

"Von don't play with me, what happened to your arm?"
I can't tell her. First she'll cry and get all stressed. Then
she'll call my momz and stress her and they'll cry together
and . . . I can't. "Did the officers do something to you?"

"Na—"

"Let me see." She grabs my arm and examines the trans-
parent stitches. "Someone cut you, didn't they? Answer
me!" Damn, I ain't never seen her this mad, I look away
avoiding her eyes because they've cut right through the

shield I've—"Von."

"Yeah Eb. I cut one of his people 'cause they tried to extort me. He wanted revenge so we went at it blade to blade. That's how it is Eb, and the way shit is goin' this damn sure won't be the last. So accept it, 'cause I have."

"Booby what's wrong with you. You gotta tell-"

"Niggas that tell get blasted every chance a nigga gets. I got two choices in here, be the prey or the predator, and I'll be damned if I let mothafuckas just run all over me." She leans across the table hugging with a grip of a python. This shit got her scared to death.

"Boo, I'm scared. I don't wanna lose you. I need you." Her voice begins the quiver which I know will lead to a stream of tears. "I don't know how I'm gonna make it through this. You didn't even do anything . . . Why is God punishing us?" I keep a low tone because I'm about to show a side of me that niggas perceive as a weakness,

"Listen, Ma this is just one more step in our future. I love you and that's what's gonna hold us down. There's gonna be a lot more shit happenin' to me in here, and we have to just accept it. I'll be alright. I'm not gonna let them take me away from you." I wipe the first tear that escapes her grasp and say, "God has a plan for us, I ain't figured out what it is yet, but I know I ain't supposed to die in here." (On the real . . . I don't believe that shit.)

The routine of this mental prison has a way of merging the days into weeks and the weeks into months. I don't know what day it is, what month—fuck it, it really don't matter. I ain't goin' home no time soon. I'm not sure how many days or weeks go by before my next fight, but like the count and chow I could always depend on it.

$ $ $ $ $ $ $ $ $ $

Again, I take that walk down the corridor leading to the dance floor. Some may think that I would be happy to be making this short journey but I'm not. I have to act like the shit that goes on here doesn't bother me. I gotta act like I don't mind spending only an hour with people I love. I don't even wanna go. The shit hurts too fuckin' much. I can see how much pain Eb and my mother are feeling. Then after an hour, I have to lock in a cell and deal with all that shit knowing I can't do anything to help them. Fuck.

As I walk in, the dark and dismal aura of the room is filled with that light. Again, a glow like no other, the officer searches for my visit to point them out, but I don't need his help. I know that glow can only be from one source, my Ebony. "Hi boo!" Her smile is intensified by that of my mothers, "Is everything O.K.?"

"I'm good." It's what my mouth says, but my eyes scream to be freed from this nightmare. Ebony takes my hand and notices the new bruises I've acquired in the past three days. These ones are from the fight with—no the semi beat, down from the E.R.U. riot squad.

"Boo what happened now? Every time we come you got some new scars."

"I'm sayin', this is jail, not summer camp. I can't not get into beef, no matter how hard I try."

"I just want you to come home in one piece."

"I'm tryin', but I can't make any promises."

"Just do what you gotta do to survive baby. Did they tell you when you're going upstate?" asks Mom.

"They don't tell us nothin'. They said I'm on some list, but it should be soon, it's been four months already."

"Did they say where you're going?" asks Mom.

"No. But once I get to a receiving facility, they'll send me whereever I'll be spending my time."

"I hope it's soon I just want this to be over already. I'm just so tired of this . . . Sean and Devin keep asking when they can come see you." Says Mom.

"I don't want them to see me in here like this."

"You'll have to see them sooner or later, you can't avoid them for too long, Boo," says Ebony.

My attention is drawn to a nigga two seats away who's watchin' me, eye contact is made and, "Yo son, you know me?"

"Yeah and I got somethin' for you for puttin' it on my cousin in the yard."

"Yeah aiight nigga, see me in the hallway."

"Fuck that, see me now muthafucka!" Suddenly he leaps up onto the knee-high plastic tables and dives at me. I manage to shield my mother from his descent as I catch him in mid flight and slam his bitch ass. My fist meets his face time and time again—once for disrespecting my mother, then for Ebony, then for me, then for the young chic and her baby sittin' next to us. Then for his girlfriend and for everyone else whose visit he fucked up. Blood explodes from his face as I do more damage to him than I did to his cousin last week. I can't even hear Ebony's and my mother's screams to stop when I stoop up and drive my visiting room slipper into the unswollen parts of his face. Quickly, several members of the *Levels* family and their co-workers tackle me and drags me to the waiting area for inmates. I calm down surprisingly quick. My plan for revenge had already been made. Luckily they all saw him jump across the table, so I won't have to do any bing time.

A calm rage engulfs my mind as I walk back to my unit, the kind of rage that's premeditated—I already know who's gonna pay for this shit. This mothafucka broke the rules. If you want beef, you wait until you get to the battlegrounds nigga; you don't disrespect the dance floor.

I reach the unit and the C.O. buzzes me in the first gate and she says, "That was kind of short."

"A nigga sent a nigga to violate me in front of my momz and girl."

"On the visit?"

I nod. "I need like three minutes of darkness."

"Say no more." She knows how I get down, and she knows a nigga violated. I walk to my cell, reach into the grooves of the locker, and remove my banger. I place it in the palm of my hand and hold it with my thumb. A nigga won't even see me slither through and blast his ass. I head for the day room, gat in hand, and ready for war. I see my punk-ass victim at a corner table playin' cards. Watch how I get his ass, I walk over smiling throwin' his whole shit off 'cause we got casual beef and says, "Yo son, let me ask you somethin'." I rest my hand on the back of his chair as his crew watches, then I whisper in his ear, "Your cousin came to see me in front of momz and girl." And I slide the razor to my fingertips with my thumb and run it from his forehead to his chin. I step back to avoid the explosion of blood that erupts from his face as the pressure from him placing his hand on the open wound causes the river of crimson red to run with ease. I swing around arm extended—razor exposed knowing his man is jumpin' up. He catches a short one from nose to cheek but it's enough to stop his tall, lanky ass. The other two niggas prepare to make their move and I yell, "One on One kid, the nigga set me up on the dance floor." Niggas' loyalty was checked at the door. The C.O. orders an immediate lock in as the victims are sent to the infirmary.

A week ago, me and this punk were playin' ball in the yard; we were on the same team. We ran a full and broke some niggas by 10 points. The next game, some niggas bet on us. This punk starts throwin' the game 'cause one of the niggas was his man, so I quit 'cause I peeped the bullshit. This punk starts flippin' on me instead of getting a new man. Then he swings and we had an even fight until he tripped and got stomped out.

As I sit on the edge of my bunk I plan my next act of vengeance, I won't be able to see money for awhile. If they sent him to the bing, I won't be . . . maybe he'll be on the floor this weekend. Yeah, I gotta stay ready. No one disrespects, my family.

The next day, my man from the upper tier comes down to kick it with me. We blaze a nice one, and he tells me how he was in the yard ballin' when he heard some Kings tellin' a kid in my house to blast me. My man is a renegade too, but the Spanish niggas respect his people on the street so they respect his position as long as he doesn't claim a set against them. This info lets me know it was time for me to move on and claim another house. I been here for four months, which is the average no ill beef run. Soon they'll be enough Kings in here for them to jump me. Then I'll have to kill a nigga. Like a true jux master, I have excellent timing and right now shit's getting hot—it's time to burn up the road.

The next day after afternoon chow, I pack up and step to the day room with my gats in hand—niggas is preoccupied—perfect setting. I creep on Bluff Daddy in complete stealth mode as if I willed myself to the point of visibility,y and with one sweeping motion, slice him from mouth to ear so clean he doesn't even feel his skin tear and part to reveal the white flesh. His brother doesn't even have time to respond to the blurry object that passes his peripheral because my razor has already found it's way to a flow that split the corner of his own mouth. The warm sensation doesn't even register in my first two victims' minds until I air out the third, causing them to grab their wounds doing more damage than before. Blood explodes and leaks like a faucet left unattended for years. I stand there guns smokin' and ready to strike again. They jump up from the table, and while two of them throw their weapons on the floor, the third tries to hold off my twin gat attack with a chair. We exchange shots a few times, then I get tired of hitting my wrist on the chair leg, so I holster a hamma. The gushing blood makes him weak, and as I pull the leg of the chair, it gives way and I slice one of his hands. He drops the chair and buoof! One swipe extends a white line from the back of his neck, through his ear, across his cheek, and ends at his mouth. Truly a work of art. I back up realizing my work is done and stumble on a body. My man laid a nigga out who tried to sneak me. So I make sure he remembers this day and give him a few lines across the face—about 17.

Quickly a nigga scans the zone lookin' for retaliation and in the far corner is all my other enemies arming themselves. I know the squad is on the way, so all I gotta do is hold them off till they get here. I turn and say, "All yall niggas that claimed to be down with me better gun up, or I'm comin' for you next, "Before I could pick another victim, doors are slamming—the turtles. I stash my guns and I'm dragged out, with a few of my sons. The bootleg Halle looks out for me and tells the Sgt-in-charge that they all attacked me, and she didn't see me cut anyone. Back to the receiving bullpens.

The receiving room looks like a police station with three large cells, large enough to hold at least 40 niggas. Me and my two sons are in one cell, and my blood soaked victims are in the other, and we're laughing at the All Mighty Latin Kings—it was three to one, and they went out like suckas. A black C.O. comes to our cell to make the report with a camera and says, "Yo, you a crazy nigga. You got a lot of heart takin' on those Kings." I don't respond to niggas ridin' my nuts. "You hurt?" I look at him like he's fuckin' stupid,

"Well act like it, 'cause the Cap that's comin' is a King on the low. Once he sees all of his people tossed up, and you ain't hurt, the situation'll be out of my control 'cause he's got the pull in this buildin'." I take my shirt off, and he starts snapping pictures from all angles.

Minutes later, the undercover King Captain comes through screaming, "You gonna pay for this. You punk mothafucka. You think you can go around cuttin' people in my building." I tell him I don't know shi. I'm just tryin' to get out of this buildin'. He walks away cursin' in Spanish, and I know I got a problem. Even if he wasn't a King, he'd be pissed off that some black kid cut up his people. Imagine havin' beef with the inmates and C.O.'s. Imagine how hard it is to protect yourself.

An hour later, a C.O.'s tellin' me and my sons to go back to the same side of the buildin'. I start yellin' that, that was straight-up homicide. This niggas tryin' to get us killed. Once we go back to the same area, all the Kings and Nietas gonna know what happened, which means they gonna be on the hunt. I refuse to leave the cell until I realize I'm goin' out like a sucka. If I'ma go—I'm goin' in a blaze of glory or I'm a figure away to walk away from it.

It's lights out and I'm in a dorm upstairs from the house of the bloodbath. This one has no cells, just a big room with 50 beds in it. Ain't no way in the world I'm sleepin' here tonight. I sit on the edge of the bed tryin' to plan an escape to the inevitable drama. My mind races along the tracks of destruction, and I notice three Spanish niggas walking to the bathroom and one keeps lookin' back at me. Shit's about to get thick. They whisper back and forth for a few minutes. Then one walks over to me and says, "Was you in the house where all those Spanish cats got cut at?" I'm silent, gat semi-exposed—planning on taking advantage of his stupidity. I say, "I don't know what you takin' about." He walks away and again the whispering starts. Next thing, I know he comes back this time talkin' loud and sayin' nothin'. The c.o. in the bubble looks around and before he can turn the lights on I splash big mouth down the middle of his face. I bounce to the bubble and the c.o buzzes me out. Back to the receiving room in less than an hour. Mission accomplished. They gotta move me now.

I maintain in the same cell I was in minutes ago. A porter comes through mopping the area, and I know his face. I look at his scar—not my artwork. I look again. It's my man from the East Side, "Yo Black, what up?"

"Chillin' baby."

"Yo, a nigga goin' to H.D.M., give me somethin' nice." He looks around, removes an 8 inch ice pick with tape on the handle from the bucket, and slides it under the cell door. H.D.M. is the illest—the two gats I got wrapped and stuffed won't be enough. I slide the ice pick up the pant leg of my fatigues and tie the drawstring to secure it.

The C.O.'s prepare me for transport so I gotta get strip searched. They move me to a shower area, and just when they turn their backs to activate the x-ray machine, I slide the pick out and it disappears under the blanket I'm standing on. They run my clothes and property through the machine, checking for weapons. My two escorts start talk-

ing about some chic and again my talent of unseen execu-
tions falls into perfection.

H.D.M. *I enter the bullpen and I'm greeted by a true*
renegade, Mike from Red Hook. This nigga is straight loco,
when I first met him he was on the run—he was wanted on
a double murder. He beat that charge even though he did it.
The day we met, I was near Bronx River Projects on the low
casin' out this crack spot. I was sittin' on the hood of a car
when Mike comes running down the block chasin' two kids
down the middle of the street, lettin' off shots at them—AT
THREE O'CLOCK IN THE AFTERNOON! The nigga hit
both of them, but they wasn't dead and he ran out of bullets
and asked me for a gun to finish the job. Of course because
he asked me, the niggas think he knows me so I had to let
him finish them off so I wouldn't have beef. After that, the
nigga was always a reliable triggerman.

Now the nigga's telling me how he just blew it up in the
four buildin'. He's waiting to be housed too. This nigga is a
real cowboy, a rebel without a cause. I take phones so I can
talk to chics to get trees, and maintain power. This nigga
takes phones just for the hell of it, and buss how he ain't
even got anyone to call. He told me he had to toss his gat so
I give him one of mine. It'll only be a matter of days before
all 7 buildin' on the Island will know there's a green light on
me. And I'm glad Mike is around 'cause I know his trigga
got heart, not because he got love for me, but because he
loves beef like a redneck trucker. So the game don't stop.

The C.O. escorts us down the corridor to our new unit.
It's just after morning chow so death is on the move like a

two-day thundering rain blessing from the hustling god. It's all good though 'cause me and Mike are in the same dorm.

We stand at the entrance and I look up at the 4 tiers with 20 occupied cells on each—it's like a four-story labyrinth of death. Imagine being able to compact 80 niggas on four 14-inch-wide platforms, in a hollow tile-lined fortress of self-destruction. Welcome to H.D.M.

There's four phones, two for black and two for Spanish. Mike and I are on the same side too. While we wait to be assigned cells, Mike starts shoutin' out cell numbers and askin' niggas who runs the phone and they better drop it like it's hot if he ends up on their cell block. Mind you, we ain't even been assigned a cell yet. The kid who runs shit on this side comes to the gate to see who's making all the noise. My man tells him, "Yo kid, you better lose that phone." Money's got no response.

We end up on the same block—we don't even go to our cells. Mike hands me the phone and, "Blow it up." I dial Niecy and my hand begins to tremble like I'm 90 years old. Adrenaline begins to rush through my veins like a freight train to hell; it's on again. Niecy's askin' me what's wrong but I keep the convo simple. I gotta stay focused. My heart is exploding through my rib cage. We just walked in and jumped on the jack with no conversation, complete psycho mode. This nigga could have 30 niggas with him and we don't give a fuck. The tension's beyond thick, shit is titanium alloy. I'm watchin' the niggas watchin' me, their nothin' but stone killas, I can see it in their eyes.

My man walks back to my side, and I try to pass off to

bring the heat down a few notches but, "Na, go ahead, rock nigga." He pulls out the ice pick and a razor I didn't even know he had, "Don't worry about nothin'." The kid who's got the jack is on the second tier lookin' down at me, I hit him with crazy shade—non-existing shade. Niecy and I ain't even talkin', I'm just listenin' to her breathe.

Mike taps me bringing my attention to three approachin' gun-totin', got-heart 'cause they're three-deep clowns. Mike says, "I'll take 'em."

If Mike says he can take 'em, he can but I can't let him have all the fun. I hang up and release the ice pick from its cage. The phone area isn't large enough for all three of them to surround us, and only two of them can attack at once. Mike wastes no time in bringing the blaze to them.

The first vic is on Mike's right and tries to jig him with a plexiglas dagger. Mike rams his left-handed pick through his forearm as he grazes the second guys face with the razor. Mike holds the first guy hostage. He's immobilized by the penetrated ice pick. He then makes three quick incisions around his eye before removing the pick and kicking him to the side. As he charges his third victim, he dodges the reckless razor swing from victim number two and pierces his rib cage two quick time with his left, and spins right taking out the pick causing a flow to fill the tier. Victim number three backs away. He's already lost. He stabs at air in fear that this carnivorous creature in front of him will only be infuriated by a punctured lung. Mike releases the blood from his arm every time he reaches for death. Finally, he reaches too far and the pick finds its way to his cheek and searches his mouth for cavities. The phone is ours.

$ $ $ $ $ $ $ $ $ $ $

Three days later, I'm on my way to court. I hadn't reported to my P.O. in six months which is a violation. Today's hearing is just a formality. I know I'm on the next thing smokin'.

Once again, I find myself in the receiving room—court bound. For transport, niggas is handcuffed to each other—the shit is dangerous for niggas like me. You get called according to the order the files are in, which means you ain't got no control over who you get cuffed to.

The C.O. calls this big 250 six and change giant, I know he's a King—the tattoo of a crown on his neck gave his stupid ass away. With my luck, I'll end up . . . "Wilson." Shit, like I ain't got a enough fuckin' problems. Now I gotta ride with this mothafucka cuffed to me. Damn. It's all good. I'm strapped. The mothfucka's ranting and raving about how he doesn't want to be cuffed to a moreno. They ignore him. My heart starts racing as visions of this clown mothafuckas blood soaking his shirt formulates a plan in my mind.

We sit on the caged bus and he shittin' on me in Spanish. I picked up a little from my Dominican mommy. Now he's talkin' loud and waving the hand that's cuffed to me around in frustration. My frame ain't shit compared to his and I'm no match for his tree limbs he uses for arms. Red lines draw themselves into my arm as money flings it around. He's really tryin' to humiliate me, so he can look good in front of his peoples and I allow him to get his shine off 'cause it puts him at ease, which makes blastin' his dumb ass so much less complicated. I just wanna end up on the same floor with him, so I can air his lame ass out first chance I get.

We hit Manhattan and we're escorted to our areas and sure enough I get blessed. The back of the courtroom is an area of bullpens where we wait, one is for adults the other is for adolescents. After uncuffing u,s they call our names and send us into a cell. The c.o. locks the gate after each one of us is checked in for security reasons. Big man is already in the cell when they call me, there's like 30 niggas in here and like seven more behind me, so when I step in the pen and the gate doesn't lock—I take advantage.

I slide through the crowd like a water moccasin in its element. My gat jumps out its hiding place and directs me to the clown sittin' in the corner off point—WOP! I turn and slip through the gate just before the C.O. slams it shut and locks it. Mission accomplished. The big mothafucka screamin' about how he's gonna kill me, yatta, yatta, yatta, yatta. They put me in the cell next door with the adolescents and they start jumpin' up and down cheerin' and ridin' my nuts for what I did.

They call me for Supreme Court part 43, and the shit is short and sweet. Next stop: a New York State Correctional Facility. See ya up north.

THE BELLY OF THE BEAST

Two days later, I get a 5:30 wake up, "Yo Von, you on the draft kid?"

"What?"

"You on the draft. You're on the next thing smokin' up north."

"Damn." The day I thought I'd be fuckin' happy to see has me . . . I don't know . . . scared? I've gotten use to this twisted shit—the next stop is unknown, but fuck it, niggas say the mountains are better.

I'm put in the receiving bullpens with 50 other niggas waitin' to be what I think is handcuffed, but I'm quickly corrected. I'm waitin', patiently as always, 'cause I'm used to the bullpen therapy. I listen to all the bullshit stories from niggas who speculate on the shit they've heard. Then, there's the niggas who're on their second or third or fourth trip up north. They're stuffin' weed and dope for the trip. "Davis, Von step up." I move through the bodies of the dead-niggas with life but no souls and stand at the edge of the cell, and a C.O. moves me into a frisk position and does his job. Next, another cuffs my hands in front of me and a chain is wrapped around my waist and connected to the cuffs. He then places a black box around the connected part and secures it with a small key lock. I'm immobilized. My hands are so close to my body, I can't scratch my nuts. I know what a slave feels like being shackled, is like . . . imagine what it might feel like to be restrained physically and have it cause a psychological pain. It's like being stripped of dignity, of pride, of decency. After being mentally fucked, I'm chained at the ankle to another nigga for the two hour bus ride to Down State Correctional. Right about now—I feel like shit—worthless. God help me.

My fear sends me into a peaceful sleep, and when I wake up, the bus is pulling into the facility. I follow orders and enter the concrete structure that seems ageless. We enter the receiving room, and the shit is chaotic—c.o.'s barkin' orders, inmates beefin'. It's like a cattle auction— niggas is counted, cleaned, numbered and stored. The whole shit just becomes a blur. I feel like I'm watching myself go through torture. It's like my mind couldn't handle what was goin' on and went to another level in order to figure this shit out.

When I come back to reality, I'm in a cell. It's concrete and cold. The walls are covered with the names of the idiots who want niggas to know they were here. It looks like that wall with all those POW and dead Vietnam niggas. This shit is a testament of death. I was given a book with the rules and regulations of the facility, a pillow case, two sheets, a thin-ass state blanket, toothpaste, toothbrush, razor, a roll of toilet paper, soap, washcloth, towel, five pairs of drawers, T-shirts, and socks. I got three state green pants, three state green shirts, one sweat shirt, one state coat, and one pair of state boots, all thanks to Corcraft. Looks like this is all a nigga needs in addition to three meals a day. I thought so too.

There's a small window with iron panels that can be tilted enough for air to get in. I stand at the window looking at the moon and the night sky that's clear and calming. The scene is peaceful. If I didn't want to be here, I might enjoy the silence, but it's now a monster that creeps up my spine like black tar that has been spilled into the sea. There is no escape from this concrete prison, Ma . . . I'm sorry for putting you through this torture. I don't want anyone else to suffer with me. Would it be better to leave my brothers alone and let them grow up without the stress of having a brother, a mentor, a father figure in prison? I'm never getting out of here—there's no way—I can't see freedom . . . I'm going to die here.

Down State is the beginning of the attempt at the mental breakdown of niggas. First, we're stripped because that's one of many things that makes us unique, our taste for how we look, then we're locked in a cell for the next seven to ten days which is part of the receiving process. Niggas are vaccinated (*like those Tuskegee niggas thought they were*), filled, logged, and numbered—I'm 99A6170. From now on, I'm to be known as 99A6170. I must remember this number and carry this fuckin' ID with me at all times—failure to do so will result in lost of the bullshit-ass privileges we have.

We're locked down 23 hours a day and only allowed to come out three times for meals and once for rec. The first two days drifted away, thanks to sleep and that facility orientation. The third drags along and the fourth tests our survival skill. After the last meal between 4-5 p.m., I couldn't do anything else but dream about Ebony. On the Island, anger, rage and being in a 24 hour war zone kept me from drifting away and surrendering to my daydreams. But in this cell, where I ain't got nothin' but myself and my memories, I have no choice. The last time I saw her smile in pleasure and not masking her pain like she's been doin', was the night before I got shot.

That night after dinner and taking turns in the shower, I propped myself in front of the entertainment area. I laid out my joints as I usually do and placed the necessary drinks in arms distance. I had just picked rookies from N.C., UConn, Duke, and St. Johns and drafted them to the starting squad of the 2001 Knicks. I was into the second game of the playoffs against the Heat when Ebony started yellin', "Von, come here! Hurry up!" I pressed pause and jetted in the bedroom thinkin' she saw a water bug or somethin', instead she was standing against the far wall leaning against the dresser with one leg slightly bent and the other locked in position as she balanced on it. Her free hand rested on her hips as she stood sideways allowing me to admire her physique, particularly her well formed exquisitely sculpted butt and thighs. Her thighs were slightly exposed due to the short golden paisley printed teddy with spaghetti straps.

The room was dark except for a candle that sat on the dresser and the moonlight that snuck through the venetian blinds. The flicker of the candle added a strange soft radiant sheen to her beauty that was enhanced by the golden shimmer of the teddy. Her satin Caramel bronze complexion created an illuminated soft luster that sent a warm gentle sensation through my body. Her eyes were filled with a blissful satisfaction, as she could see from the expression on my face that she had given me a gift greater than she could ever imagine. I stood there unaware of time or the world outside of that room for what seemed to be hours, 'cause I was mesmerized by this Queen that stood before me. Noticing I was twisted, she picked up the candle and walked towards me seeming to float on a cloud of flickering light. She laid it on the nightstand and while saying, "Let the real games begin." She extinguished the light with a stroke of her hand. The moon wasn't bright enough to interrupt the silence of the darkness, but I didn't need light to see. The glow my Queen possessed was enough to lead my way.

Her slender physique and sensual walk made her appear to be a beautiful black panther searching the night for her prey. Her soft hand gently grabbed my own, and a tepid sensation changed the temperature of my body opening my pores to release the beginning of what would soon be sweat. Adrenaline began to flow causin' my heart to slightly race in excitement of the most unforgettable pleasure, which would accompany that night.

Ebony led me to the bed like a blind helpless man who lost his way, and in that darkness, she placed a kiss perfectly on my lips. Our kiss was not disrupted as we laid on the bed, and I volunteered to remove my clothes first. I wanted to have the great pleasure of listening to Ebony's reaction to my undressing method. The straps were thin as if Miss Victoria knew it would be necessary for my tantalizing plan. I placed my lips lightly on Ebony's neck as we laid on our sides with our bodies forming an S shape with me behind her. Inch by inch, my lips moved towards her shoulder, and as I reached the first strap, I nudged it to the edge and it gave way losing its grip. She knew the other strap was next, and I always start from the top and work my way down, so she rolled over on to her stomach. I began kissing her shoulder blades in the same light way as before, but with wet passion, leaving a bit of moisture with each one and again I pushed the strap to the side. Now at that point, a nigga could imagine how difficult it would be to remove the teddy without getting it snagged or stuck. Well watch my skillz. First her arms were completely freed from the straps. Then I began pulling it down on the edges making sure to push the mattress down in the spots that may stop its flow, (think about it).

Ebony's skin is beyond soft, and I always took time to show my appreciation, especially in the area where her breasts begin. Knowing the breasts are the most sensitive part of her body, I teased her by lightly breathing over their most sensitive spot, arousing her in anticipation of my kiss. Slowly my lips massaged every inch of this garden of Caramel sweetness on my way to the danger zone. Her moans revealed her desire to have me taste her essence. There is where I always showed my love for her female anatomy. She spread her thighs and I positioned myself for the journey. Slowly my tongue parted the cavern from bottom to top causing her feminine secretion to expose itself. I toyed with the center of her depth teasing enough to excite and then with no warning . . . *Fuck!*

Rage fills my heart with a piercing burning pain that knocks me from the bed to my knees in agony. Why, why am I being punished? What have I done to deserve to be put into this horrid nightmare? Does God hate me so much? Suddenly my lungs feel like they're being crushed by the hand of death. Every breath is a struggle as if it's being removed from every cell in my body. I try to call for help, but I have nothing. Then it stops as if it never happened, I can do nothing but release my fear and pain in a river of tears.

The once cherished memory becomes a nightmare because it will be a long time before I'll be blessed with such a touch by my love. The anger in me begins to swell as it has done many times in the past six months. But now I'm unable to vent my rage on those who were so easily tricked into a violent encounter to help feed the vengeance that my hate yearned for and could never satisfy. I decide that pushups and dips will help to eventually ease my frustration. I stand in the unbreakable mirror, sizing myself up between sets, and for the first time, I notice the one-inch thick scar that runs from below my windpipe to my abdomen. For the first time, I see how ugly it is; for the first time I'm hurt by the sight of this disfigurement, and I understand why Ebony cried when she said it's permanent. That punk mothafucka shot me; the nigga scarred me for life. How can I forget this—I can't, won't, I want revenge, I want him to feel the pain, I want him to suffer, I want . . . his blood. Let him bow down in gut-wrenching anguish and mind altering pain as he feels the wrath of *My Rage*.

Day 5—First day I get to take a shower since the ice cold shit in receiving. The water is lukewarm, but it's aiight for now. Today I decide to play my door. The cell has a 2 inch-by-10 inch opening. It's just big enough for me to look at the five cells in my section. We ain't got no names, just cell numbers. I'm 8 cell. four and five cell are across from me and their both bloods, young boys too, like 19-20; 9 and 6 are old timers and 7 is the foreigner he barely speaks English. four and five been talkin' since they got here, and today the loneliness plagues them both as they call out to rest of us for convo. I listen to the bullshit for rec—4 is open on 5. This nigga is tellin' us about his case and how large the nigga he worked for is. They gonna take care of him yatta, yatta, yatta—4 cell's actin' like this niggas an-up-and-comin' Alpo or Fat Cat. These niggas is goin' at it, but all I'm doin' is listening. I ain't tryin' to give no info.

Day 6—More fuckin' bullshit and stories. I'm tired of hearin' these muthafucka's mouths. All day bullshit, niggas ain't talkin' about shit hour after hour. I pace my cell, I work out, I sleep, I think about . . . Damn I miss my peoples . . . shit.

Day 7—I'M STRESSIN' THE FUCK OUT. I gotta talk to these niggas, but I don't like 'em.

Day 8—One more day, one more fuckin' day.

Day 9—Finally I'm out. I move to the rec area where the TV is on some real backwards twisted shit. I'm happy. The TV got a nigga smilin'. I ain't figured out the psychological game they just played on us, but I know it's somethin' for the books. Fuck around and it's already on the books. It's 10:00 a.m. and we'll be able to watch TV until the count and after chow. Then, at 8:00, lockdown until the next morning, so I soak this idiot box shit up.

7:50—before the lock-in they give us a pencil paper and envelopes to write letters to our peoples. I try but I can only write a few lines . . . it hurts too much to say how much . . . I love . . . damn I miss my peoples.

Day 10—"8 cell pack it up." With the swiftness I bag and bounce. These other clown niggas is tryin' say goodbye—fuck you, I'm out. "8 cell—mess hall dorm." Mess hall dorm, I don't wanna work in this muthfucka.

Day 13— "8, 10,12, 22, 30, 40. Pack it up, you're on the draft." Now I'm on my way to the spot where I'ma be doin' the rest of my bid. Once again, I'm strip- searched and shackled. On the move again.

Auburn Correctional Facility

Due to a facility error, instead of being sent to a medium security facility, which I was classified for, I'm sent to Auburn maximum security state correctional. Here the average niggas is serving anywhere from six years to life. In a medium, niggas is servin' from one to five, short time. Niggas in maxs ain't too keen on cuts who got a lot less time than they do. And medium niggas don't have serious charges, drugs, petty theft. Max—murder, rape, bank robbery. Imagine how pissed off a nigga doin' 15 or 20 to life gets when he meets a cat doin' 2 Ω-9. Believe shit won't be pretty between them. Right now I'm only 140 and a bit too cute to be in a max, and as I expect, during my first five days I'm informed by an old Muslim dude that I'd be raped by a booty bandit in the next couple of days. Now what?

The next two days I spend in my cell, wide awake. I don't even come out for chow or showers. Every booty bandit in here is two and change and can bench-press twice my weight. I've only been here a hot minute and I can't get a gat yet 'cause . . . fuck that, niggas is gonna try and rape me—I can't avoid 'em forever. I lay on my bunk as the fear that once gave me courage grows to a fear of possible failure.

When I was on the Island my mother told me, "God did what he had to do to beat the Devil, so you do what you gotta do to beat his soldiers." That night they call rec and the old Muslim walks by my cell and says, "Come on aki, you can't stay locked in your cell your whole bid." Fuck it, if I'ma go out at least I'll go out like a trooper.

I stand with the Muslim brother and he does his best to recruit another soldier for the Army of Islam. I puff on a stoge and Ak's words float off as my mind untangles itself to find an answer to my present situation. Ak's just beginning to irritate me when, "Yo that's the cat right there." I look in the direction he motions and, "The one on the bench?"

"Yeah." My heart starts racing like Ben Johnson when he became the fastest man alive. Suddenly fear is replaced again with courage and fearless rage, this muthafucka is at least 6'2 and 250 plus. All the chumps in the facility and he wants me. He thinks I'ma just let him run up in me like some bitch. Fuck that . . . show time baby. I slither through the shadow of bodies using them like a king cobra on the hunt. I pace myself as his man finishes his set and he takes his place on the bench. I can't reveal myself yet. I breeze by a weight rack and remove a five, pound plate without lookin' at it or losing sight of my victim. The booty bandit is into his fifth rep and his man stands to the side 'cause there's no spotter needed. The plate swings with my hand, calmly silently. I seem to be walking by and effortlessly I raise the weapon and bring it crashing down on his face causing an explosion of blood to erupt from below. The weight slides off his face just as I turn like nothing ever happened. From behind screams that should come from a woman escape his mouth and I smile with a grin of relief. Ain't gonna be no fuckin' tonight.

By the time I get to my cell the C.O.'s were waiting for me. Box time baby.

When the dep. found out there was an error in my transfer I was given 60 days instead of 180 and I was shipped out to a medium security. I had grounds for a lawsuit because the state's fuck up could've gotten me hurt. So they shipped me out hoping I wouldn't start no lawsuit shit, but I figure the only way to make it out of here alive is to be seldom seen and never heard.

Oneida Correctional

After the Auburn incident, I was kept locked for 15 days, then transferred to Oneida's box for the remainder of my time. I wrote Ebony and my mother two or three times a week and I didn't receive any answer from anyone. I ain't speak to them since I was at Downstate a month ago.

The box in this facility is bigger than a cell, and instead of bars, it has a steel door with a window. After the routine beat down by the duty officers, I'm placed in 10 cell, and further referred to as such. I'm locked in again for 23 hours a day and let out only for one hour in a small cage for my required state recreation. All my meals are brought to me, and once a week I'm entitled to a book, and twice a week I get a shower. Besides the officers bringing me meals and the birds that have a nest outside my window, I'm totally cut off from life. One never realizes how important human contact is until it is taken from you. The mind begins to desire conversation and as it speaks to itself or you talk to yourself. You begin to project personalities on inanimate objects. A nigga don't think the object is actually talkin' but you will think for it. Basically you talk to the sink or the bed, because you have no one else to talk to.

Being that I was not getting any response to my letters, twisted nightmares became a reality. The facility has a way that they torture niggas when they want—one tactic is they stop mail from leavin' the facility. The shit just gets fuckin' lost. I was givin' letters to the officers, and they weren't even sendin' them out, but I thought Eb was just not answering the letters. So imagine how crazy I've become. The main reason I was cut off was because of my grounds for a lawsuit. If I would have gotten hurt due to the misplacing of my security classification I would have been able to sue, something they could not have. So for 53 days, unknown to me, my peoples had no idea where I was. I thought I was left for dead—almost every night images of Ebony in the arms of another man eat away at my mind and insanity slowly creeps up on me.

As I lay again in my bunk, my mind blank and watching the birds like a man whose life is near end, the officer bangs on the door and tells me to get ready for a visit. Totally lifeless and full of hate, I am emotionless as I'm escorted to a caged minivan with my hands in my pocket for safety.

I enter the visiting room, and as always, the glow that fills it comes from only one source, but today it doesn't fill me with warmth. This time it sends my cold heart into the depths of a frozen hell. Ebony received a letter that was 30 days old and rushed to the facility hoping she was not sent on another of the four wild goose chases she's been through in search of me. I'm covered in facial hair, pale from lack of sun, and I'm in the worse condition I've been in since the hospital. The sight of me brings tears of pain and relief to her eyes. "Von we were so worried about you. I thought you were dead. You didn't call, you didn't write. We called every facility in New York looking for you, and no one knew anything. What happened?"

"What happened? I was in the box, that's what happened. I wrote crazy letters and you and my momz never answered one of them. Why? What, you found another nigga or something? What the fuck is goin' on? I been in the box almost two fuckin' months and you and my momz ain't come through once."

"What, no I'm not with anyone . . . Von why are you saying that, and we ain't get any letters from you. I just got one Thursday and it had last month's date on it. Come on you know I would've-"

"Bullshit Eb I wrote 24 letters and y'all ain't get any of them. You think I'm fuckin' stupid. The least y'all could've done was let a nigga know he's cut off."

"What!—What are you talkin' about, we been going crazy lookin' for yo ass and now I come up here and I gotta listen to this shit. Fuck that, you call me when you've had some time to think!" And she storms away leaving me with no more answers to my questions. The C.O.'s have accomplished their mission.

$ $ $ $ $ $ $ $ $ $ $ $ $

The following weekend Ted comes to see me. I got out the box two days before, and I'm beginning to improve. I enter the room looking for my mother or Ebony, and I'm confused because they're missing. Then I see a hand raised that is connected to a huge body, my man Big Ted Boogie.

With no shame I hug my man and the tree limbs he calls arms almost crush my spine. "What's up my nigga? I heard you was in the box kid."

"Yeah 60 days, I just got out Thursday, shit had me fucked up too. I was goin' crazy—yo, I was talkin' to the walls and toilet 'n shit. I thought momz duke bounced on me and Ebony was with some other nigga. Yo, she came up and I flipped on her. And I'm still on lost of privileges so I can't call them and try to fix shit."

"I'm sayin' you know she wouldn't do no shit like that."

"I don't know, I'm in here and she's out there. I only know what she tells me."

"Yo, you think she's fuckin' with someone else? I'm sayin', Ebony loves you like crazy. She ain't tryin' to replace you nigga. Almost every day, she's at Gwen's crib and she spends the night so fuckin' much, she's got her own toothbrush. The whole time you were missin', Gwen stayed with her, and all she did was talk about you and how she couldn't imagine ever seein' you again. She's been with you every step of the way through this whole shit, and you think she'd come all this way to fuck with some lame nigga. Fuck all that other shit. You think I'd let her have some cat up in your crib and pushin' your ride. Come on, nobody around the way's gonna let shit like that ride."

"True. I don't know Ted. This jail shit's got me fucked up . . . I'm losin' it and I know I'm spazin' out. I'm flippin' on the only woman who rode this wave with me, next to my momz."

"Yo, write her and tell her what's goin' on, and the shit you're goin' through. I'll tell Gwen to smooth shit out a bit to help her understand."

"Good lookin'. Yo, did you ask Gwen to marry you yet?"

"No."

"Why? What happened?"

"You got locked up. We were suppose to do it together remember."

"I'm sayin'—"

"I ain't tryin' to hear you. I got both rings waitin' and ain't nothin' goin' down until you get home cuzin'."

"Yo kid—. . . I'm sayin'.

"I know—me too." A silence fills me and my man as we get our emotions under control. This place is nowhere to be shedding a tear.

As always the visit is too short and I don't want to see my man go, but that's the way shit goes.

As Ted begins his five-hour drive back to the world, he reflects on his v.i. with his best friend. When the visit was over it was hard for him to leave his man, not only because he missed him but because he had become a part of his and Gwen's life, and he was leaving a piece of his existence in that room. He picks up his cell and dials Gwen's office, "Hello Gwendolyn Pierce."

"Yeah it's me."

"Hey Teddy, where are you? I thought you were going to visit Von."

"I just left I'm on my way back." *She can sense something's wrong with the usual joyful man in her life,* "What's wrong?" *she asks and for a moment the phone is silent as he tries to control his feelings enough to express them,* "Yo . . . he looks bad Gwen. They're suckin' the life right out of him. Every time I see him he seems to be getting colder and colder, you know . . .and . . .it's like the nigga I got love for is slowly dying and I can't do anything to help him." *For the first time in their relationship, she has no words which can begin to comfort the man who has always been there when she needed.* "And the fucked up part about it is it could've been me behind the wall and him comin' to visit. I could be as easily taken hostage as he was for some crazy shit. You could be the one crying yourself to sleep every night 'cause I'm gone, and there wouldn't be shit we could do about it." *Tears start to release themselves from both their eye. Ted feels the pain of his fallen fellow solider, and Gwen has just been faced with the possibility of her worse nightmare.* "Yo umm . . . when you get back to the house, call Eb and try to smooth shit out for Von. He said something that pissed her off. He said he's gonna write her but do me a favor and talk to her, aiight?"

"O.K. Teddy be careful driving back."

"I will."

"I love you."

"I love you too." *Neither of them hang up for fear that the connection they have may be broken as the fear of losing each other lays heavy on their minds, but finally Gwen gets the courage to sever the line.*

After the visit with Ted, I make moves back to the dorm—I gotta write this letter. This shit with Eb is tearing me apart. Anger no longer fills me when I think about her, and because she is a part of me and I've pushed her away, I'm totally incomplete.

Ebony walks into the apartment she still refuses to call

home until her love is returned to her, and sits in his favorite chair, as she has done every day since he was taken from her. She's had to do things to help her keep him fresh in her mind because she's afraid if she doesn't envision him or his touch or scent, it would be the beginning of her getting used to him being gone, something she fears more than him never returning to her.

The communication they once had was something she always described as spiritual. Many times he was unable to express to her how upset he was and yet she always understood. It was a sensation she could feel in her uterus like the growth of a child. If he was near, she could feel his presence, even if she didn't know he was around. The first day she saw him in front of that club, she knew she was going to be in love. Even when she tried to pull away from him because she felt she was falling too fast and hard, she found herself longing for and being drawn back to his love. Now just when they were beginning to go in the direction she always hoped for, Von was snatched from their world and it seemed to take a turn for the worse.

She hopes they will be able to stay strong through this ordeal, but more, and more she sees him changing into something she doesn't understand. The man she fell in love with is deep beneath this monster that has taken over. Ebony is hurt and terrified, but there's no way she's going to let him get away that easy. Whoever this person is who has invaded and taken over the body of the man she loves doesn't know this black Queen is going to fight for her soul mate's life with every inch of her being, and if that's not enough, then with her very last breath, and if that's not enough, with her last drop of blood, and still if she cannot defeat this beast, then she'll have no choice but to call on the assistance of Von's mother.

She sorts through the mail praying for a message from her love, she knows he has to take the first step to help her begin this battle. She sees a letter addressed to Mrs. Ebony Mitchell written in the only handwriting she can distinguish from any other, and it fills her with a momentary joy. She spends several minutes absorbing the love she can sense from the way the first letter of her name is larger then the rest. Von always said the way someone writes the first letter of someone else's name is what shows how they feel about you. If they write your name the same way they write their own, they feel you're their equal. She opens the letter as delicately as she possibly can and as she removes the pages she just realizes how beautiful his handwriting is. He never writes in script, only when he signs his name, his print is more an artsy graffiti type. All the words are slanted in the same direction and it's as if the words represent his speech because the most important words are slightly larger and more elongated than the others.

Dear Ebony,

When I first began writing this letter, I apologized for my behavior for almost two pages. Then I realized, for me to apologize for something that is not my fault and I didn't realize I was doing, would be like lying to you. I also knew you would forgive me because you love me but you would never forget. I decided I would try my best to help you understand the psychological torture I'm going through. I don't fully understand it myself, so some of this may sound crazy. One thing I do know about us is we truly do feel each other and in some odd way, our souls seem to be on the same page when communicating with one another.

First off, understand that I'm in a demonic world where showing any other emotion than anger, rage, manipulation, and abuse will cause you to be mentally or physically destroyed. Violence and bloodshed are the only way to solve problems. The only reason for a discussion is to determine the place where the bloodshed will occur. In order for me to survive, I have had to suppress all the good in me and create and unleash the monstrous persona you have come to know. I have had to turn myself into the very thing I hate the most in life. Now, because I have been this person day and night I have forgotten how to be the person I once was. I forgot how to be kind, caring, warm, and considerate. I forgot how to smile and laugh. I forgot how to feel good. I have become used to misery and making those around me miserable as well, because here, one who is happy is weak, and must be taken advantage of. Being used to being miserable also caused me to push love away from me. You love me so much, and I have to return the same thing to you because it feels wonderful, but I can't afford to feel love and lose focus of the war around me because it may cost me my life.

When I went to the box my mind began to warp. Being alone in a room for almost two months literally drove me crazy. Not only was I talking to myself, but I was talking to everything else as well. I wrote you letters three times a week, and at first I thought the facility was holding my mail, then the crazier I became the more I began doubting your love. Yes this does sound crazy but you must understand I was not able to think rationally.

Ebony, I know you love me and I don't know how I could ever doubt you, and I know you can feel the love I will always have for you. Right now, I'm going through some real deep shit and no one can help me behind these walls. All you can do for me now is try to bare with my psychotic behavior until I figure a way to fix myself. This situation is as painful for me as it is for you. Yes I too feel the heartache I put you through and I hate myself for it, and if it gets too bad, I'll understand if you don't want to take it any more and decide to move on and try to forget about me. I would be hurt but I would understand. I want you to be happy so don't feel guilty if you decide to make that move. I will always love you no matter what, and I need you more than the air I breathe. Please understand and don't let the monster I have become make you hate the man I once was and whom you love.

I love you, Von

As she reads the last words of the letter, the pain which fills the pages is expressed through her tears for the strength her love possesses. As all odds are against him, he not only worries about himself but her as well. She could never leave him, no matter how crazy he became and how horrid the situation becomes, she knows she must be as strong as he is, in order to help him as she's prepared to do so. She folds the tear-soaked pages back into the three quarters and places it in the envelope it came in. Then just as she begins to control the river from her eyes she places her hand on the very spot where she felt the sharp pain when Von was shot and says, "Don't worry, we'll make it through this."

$ $ $ $ $ $ $ $

I think it's been like 4-5 months since I got out the box. I don't know exactly because knowing how long you got left drives you straight up the wall. The shit makes the time go a lot slower, so not knowing how long it's been makes the whole experience seem like one long week or month. It's hard to know when something happened, so on the real, if you can't tell how much time has passed, imagine how I feel forcing myself to do the same thing. I'm just waiting for the day the C.O. calls me and tells me to pack up 'cause I'm on my way back to the world.

After the box, I was sent to a reception dorm for a hot minute, then to L dorm. These two stick-up kids I went to high school with were there. Instantly I was recruited to the Harlem clique, which consisted of us three and one more cat from the Bronx. Trig, Ched, and Bolo. Trig was the instigator with a short left hand that could drop just about any nigga. Ched, short for Chedda, he's the money man—"if it ain't about the doe, then let that shit go." Bolo's the Chinese nigga who's black under that yellow skin. Then there's me, Von—The Chef. Niggas ain't really start callin' me that until the first bloody incident with the four of us took place.

It was like two days after I started runnin' with niggas. Me and Bolo were in the day room talkin' about different martial art techs and who had the best styles, the Chinese Japanese, or Cantonese. This undercover chump had lent Bolo a tape and the chump said, "Yo Bolo what's up with my mix tape?"

"I got it, you want it?" said Bo.

"Yeah." Said the Chump.

"Aiight. Let me finish talkin' to my man and I'll get it." Said Bo.

"What? Yo I wanna rock now!" said the Chump. Now we know this homo nigga was tryin' to play my man. See I was new to the dorm and the chump didn't know my status so he made a move by tryin' to clown Bolo by orderin' him to do somethin'. Bolo is a live nigga and the chump thought if he could snatch Bolo's heart for a quick minute, I'd show him respect, or I'd be down with him.

Bolo got stuck for a minute and that was all I needed to jump up and unleash my metallic beast. The first incision went from his eye to the back of his jaw line, the second was from his ear to his nose. Bolo was surprised at the swiftness of my guns, from then on the Chef has lived.

With my new niggas also came new ways to vent my frustrations, the juvenile behavior we engaged in was a fun way to do harm to others to feed our hunger for vengeance. Razor tag became our favorite game—slice across the face and you it. Unlike me, my niggas didn't have families that took care of them so they had to find other ways to live in jail. Extortion was our favorite, the sight of blood flowin' from the faces of one of our many nonpaying victims became the norm. But soon it wasn't enough to tame the raging beast called Pain, and we had to find other games.

L dorm became a house of horrors as the four of us became restless. An idle mind is the devil's playground. I don't know who said that shit, but they was right on the fuckin' money.

My first truly bloody incident was in the yard—I was buyin' some trees from some homo nigga and he tried to get fly with the mouth talkin' about how cute I was and how he'd love to taste me inside of him. I wasted no time lacin' his faggot ass with two quick doctor like incisions from ear to chin and from forehead to jaw. My hand speed and precision had developed greatly on the Island and the more I practiced, the more I impressed myself.

Time and time again, we terrorized the weak and strong and with the reputation, we became somewhat of living legends. But we were still not happy.

$ $ $ $ $ $

The facility has mandatory program movement, and every day we'd all go to the gym. Trig and Ched played ball, and Bolo and I worked out. Bolo used to watch niggas ball until I came, but then he found a workout partner. The first month we worked out haphazardly. Then an old timer got down with us and put us on to the proper shit. The nigga was down like 18 joints, and he said I reminded him of his little brother who got shot in a number-hole stick up. So he wanted to look out for me and Bo. It made him feel good so we let him live. Then one day I heard some Dogs talkin' about how they were gonna eat his food, 'cause Pops clowned him in the gym. I told my people Pops was cool with me, and I wasn't havin' it. The Bloods were like 30 strong in the facility but half were in the box. But I really ain't give a fuck. So the game was set.

The one I heard talkin' shit was in my house so I slid up to his cube and, "Listen Dog, you got beef with an O.T. that held me down, so you got beef with me. Either me and you can take it to the yard and go gun to gun, or you can bring three of your brothers with you. Or you can let it ride, it's on you."

"I'll bring three to hold me down."

"On the 8:00 movement."

"Aiight."

"8:00, attention all radio holders, attention all radio holders, run the 8:00 movement, 8:00 movement run 'em out." My four-man clique moves with war on the mind and gats in boot. Sometimes they have random searches at the gym, but all they do is a pat down frisk—like no one hides shit in their boots, dumb-ass mountain boys. We arrive in the yard first and take position in plain view so we can be seen by our victim. Now, any assembly with more than five inmates is considered unauthorized or gang intended. So each one of us is accompanied by one and the rest stand watch for C.O.'s and snitches.

The Dog who wants the ruckus, sheds his state coat like I do, even though this mountain air is crisp and icy hard. It's like cave man, ice-age Antarctic in January cold—some ole' hypothermia, mad 'cause you brought your dumb-ass outside shit. I ain't tryin' to be out here more than like three minutes any way, so I skip pass the convo, pull the gat and take it to him. I go for a facial incision, and money blazes the back of my hand, nicely too. I smile because it's been awhile since I've had a worthy opponent.

The first one was on the Island, a young renegade kid. We went at it for like 15 minutes—the only reason we stopped was 'cause niggas were both bleeding too much. We ended up cool too.

I decided it's time to step up the game. I play hand games with money by stickin' out the left and retuning the bloody favor when he goes for the slice. One for one. We swing at air only because both of our skills won't allow any more. Then he leaves his hand out a little too long after he attempts a body slice and I grab him by the wrist. A nigga drags the razor across his knuckles to weaken his grip. Then when he reaches to grab my wrist, I hit him with an upward stroke like a blood thirsty Devincci opening his palm, and he regrets his slowness. Because I got respect for money's blade game I don't bless him with a facial deformity, but I do give him a few quick ones on the hands so he'll never forget. I release the bloody hand and, "I respect y'all niggas, that's why it was one on one and strictly hands. Shit is squashed between us."

"No doubt."

My wounds were barely leakin' but his needed treatment. We walked out into the clearin' and Bo and I breezed inside just as the C.O. snatched up Trig, Ched, and the 4 Dogs—the bloody Dog couldn't hide his wounds and when the c.o saw him, the shit was over. Next thing I heard they were all getting transferred out of the facility and the Bloods wouldn't snitch so nobody could get box time. There goes the clique.

A few days after, part of my squad got transferred. Pops rolled up on me in the dorm and said, "Yo youngblood, I heard what you did, and you did it without lettin' a brother know. That let me know it was official. I take care of my peoples." And he walked away. Three days later, he went down on a visit. When he came back, he blessed me with two balloons. He said if I didn't smoke just pass 'em off. After that every time he came back from a v.i. he was blessin' me with trees.

Bolo and I lived love with the free trees and my packages, and except for the occasional game of razor tag, we were able to subdue our rage with the help of the herbal tranquilizer, and a flashback to our days on the street. We knew it wouldn't last forever, but we ain't give a fuck; a nigga gotta live for the moment when shit is fucked up.

Pause

It's been eight months ago I got out the box and ever since the letter, Eb has had a different understanding of the whole shit, and it's made her more concerned and protective. She's been coming to see me every weekend and it's really fuckin' with me. I don't like to be a strain on people I love. It's a five-hour drive to the facility and she does it regularly with total dedication. She wants me to call every other day but each call is almost 15 dollars for 25 minutes, and usually all we talk about is what's goin' on beyond my reach. Needless to say, I told her I was only goin' to call once a week. She's paying the bills alone. I ain't tryin' to make it harder than it already is so when she comes to visit, I try to make shit smooth.

"Ebony I want you to stop comin' up so much. I still got a year and some change left on this bid and it'll be easier if you come like once or twice a month instead of every week."

"Easier for who? For you or me? It's not gonna be easy on me. You know how hard it is for me to sleep in our bed alone—the first six months you were gone, I slept on the couch. I can't do anything without thinking about you. I need you Von. I need these visits. I'm not coming up here because you want me to. You don't think I thought about cutting down?"

"I love you, but comin' here is expensive, and runnin' up the phone bill with collect calls doesn't help."

"Listen, you think being a man is about sacrificing these visits to help me. Well you're wrong. This is pure selfishness. Stop thinking about how you feel and think about what these little eight-hour visits mean to me!"

"I just feel—"

"Yeah, yeah, you feel—well I'm not gonna stop comin', and if you stop callin', I'm telling your mother so cut the shit! It's time for you to sacrifice that little feeling."

"Damn. If I didn't know you, I'd think you was about to leave me."

"Never that, and don't think you're getting rid of me that easy."

"Yeah aiight, I love you too. I just don't want to see you

suffering."

"I know, and that's what makes me love you more."

"I just hope this shit doesn't fuck us up when I get out."

"As long as we stay true to the love we have, we'll always make it."

"Love can heal all this shit?"

"That's the only thing that can heal the wounds that this situation causes."

"You sound like my momz."

"Where you think I got it from?"

5

THE WORSE NIGHTMARE

Niggas in jail ain't got nothin' but time and the first few months I was here, I always knew what the date was, but now I don't care and I don't care about how long I been here—I just wanna go the fuck home. Really, I can't even think about—all I know is it's been like 20 somethin' months—20 somethin' months too fuckin' long.

Once again, the sun creeps through the cracks of my window disturbing my slumber, and I open my eyes to see the figure of the woman I love more than life itself. Quickly I defy the sun's commands and continue to feel the warmth from the love of Ebony's cuddling touch. I smell her scent, which is almost like a pleasant form of ether, which helps to return me to my peace. I open my eyes again, this time to darkness, and suddenly I realize I'm still in a squeaky bunk in a mental hell.

I sit up and rub my eyes tryin' to clearly focus on the clock that lays on the wall near the bubble. Again it reads

4:30. My thoughts run back along the time-line of this fucked up life I've been dropped in and some how a nigga has changed again. At one time, I was like a reckless rene-gade nigga who whyled out every chance I got, but now . . . it's like I've become a great nocturnal jungle beast who is unseen until it's time to strike. I'm like a genetically enhanced predator. These niggas in here don't have the intelligence to fuck with a nigga like me. I can move amongst them and destroy at will, and they can't do shit about it. I have become a chameleon-like demon with loy-alties to no one but myself. I am The Chef of Blood.

Darkness still fills the sky as I begin my daily routine. I grab my toothbrush from my locker and lace it with the dragon tamer. I put on sweatpants and sneakers and reach for my banger out of pure instinct, then I realize I don't need it this early in the morning because everyone's still asleep. I remove the chair from the cube's entrance, which is strategically set up as a blockade and warning for unwant-ed guests. I walk pass each cube avoiding lookin' into any specific one. Somehow I've learned to respect a nigga's pri-vacy, and I ain't tryin' to see no perverted sexual acts. I close in on the bubble and the C.O.'s are fast asleep. Two more possible victims if I so desired.

After relieving myself, I continue my ritual. During the roughest months, I've been avoiding making eye contact with the person looking back at me. He's a reflection of the monster I've become. The once perfect sculpted blowout done by Kazo like barber is now a reflection of my anger. My Caramel sun-coated, unblemished skin is dry unhealthy and discolored due to the hard water and lye-infested Corcraft soap. Dark circles have formed under my eyes from a less-than-perfect sleep, not from the stress that one may believe, but from the possibility of my blood being shed. I return to my cube in full stealth mode, something I'm unable to control at this stage in my bid. I now have a need to be unseen until I choose, a true asset.

Four forty-five, in and hour an fifteen minutes, the lames will be wakin' up for the day, and I hate being up when they're movin' around. I can't stand to be that fuckin' close to a nigga whose every word makes my fuckin' skin' crawl, whose very presence is infuriating, who's total existence is worthless. From my cube, I can look out the window that's directly across from me. The night is still beautiful even though my view is distorted by the steel gate that covers it.

Ebony was the only woman whose electrifyingly pure natural essence could be compared to the dynamic captivating creation that is the clear night sky. I know we'll someday be together, but I still can't ease the raging flame of torturing pain that fills my heart 'cause I can't feel her touch. My head hangs heavy into my hands for a moment too long, and I hear the C.O. make the call and say, "O'Neal, L dorm 51 in, 51 out." Now I only have an hour before the wake-up so it's time to put my mind at ease to pray not to dream of my love 'cause it will only bring another day of mind-melting fury.

"On the chow." Is nothing but a mere whisper tickling my ears as I return to a shallow sleep. Fifteen minutes later, the dorm explodes into a frenzy of loud obnoxious empty conversations. The fuckin' lames always come back from chow makin' too much fuckin' noise. Every fuckin' day, the same fuckin' shit, day in day. Out why the fuck can't they be quiet just once. "Yo on the fuckin' noise, mothafuckas is tryin' to sleep." Niggas bring shit down to a low murmur. They know my shit is dangerous when unleashed, and if I gotta blow my cool, niggas will surely pay in blood.

"Attention all radio holders, run the morning program, programs run 'em out." Eight o'clock, mandatory program movement. This is the facility's way to get us to work for pennies. I ain't like these other niggas. I refuse to work in the mess hall or commissary or as a porter because slavery was abolished hundreds of years ago, and I'll be damned if I give these ex-farm boys turned C.O.'s the benefit of actin' like an overseer. So it's gym time.

Last month, Bolo took a job in the mess hall so he's on the other side of the facility, so now I meet him in the gym. I make moves into the frigid weather of the mountain and it let's me know I'm far from home, so I tighten up the state coat and flip up the collar on the chino to protect my neck. The chino is state issued but I bought it from my man who works in the state shop for four packs of Newports. He sold it to me right off his back. It's been altered so the collar is longer than average and I couldn't resist it. The Harlem nigga in me was drawn to the steelo that separates us from the rest of the world. Later I peeped how the jacket served another purpose.

The walkways that lead through this wasteland of hate are filled with niggas durin' mandatory movement, and it can be a dangerous zone for a nigga who's got beef. There aren't enough C.O.'s to watch us all, and if you've ever been on 34th street durin' the day or in the train station durin' rush hour, then you know someone can be cut and stabbed four-five times before anyone even notices. Back on the Island, I got in a lot of drama and in Auburn, before I was transferred, and one thing I learned, you always run across the same niggas on your tour of these jails. Whenever you have a problem at one spot, they just move you to another jail and then maybe back to that same jail later so you always have to remember faces. Now as I walk to the gym in this mob, it's hard to peep everyone so a nigga gotta transform and camouflage. The collar on the chino covers the lower half of my face. My state coat distorts my actual size, and the scully is pulled down so low my eyes are almost invisible. This, in addition to my stealth capabilities, makes me non-existent. My Harlem shine needs to be well cloaked so I blend right into the sea of state greens.

I move through the crowd like a two-door Ac floatin' in and out of traffic on the Westside Highway . . . The Westside Highway . . . me and Ted always raced on the Westside on the late night comin' home from a hot spot. Gwen and Ebony use to gas us up knowin' we would challenge each other; somethin' about speed drove them crazy. After the race, they were all charged up and . . . Shit! Gotta stay on point, can't afford to let a bandit get too close, fond memories can cost a nigga his life.

The gym is crowded like always. I sign in and move to the weight room where my man Bo is today. We're doin' chest so he's got a bench locked down. Me and Bolo are both out cast in this cesspool of hate. I'm a nigga who had love in his heart and in his world and is now forced to mask it with a monstrous persona and as one whose shine is official. I gotta separate myself and hide from the hatas that would end my life or scar me just because. Bolo's Japanese and was raised in the Bronx and relates more to niggas than his own kind and in here neither of them accept him. "What's the word Bo?"

"Peace Sun."

"Temporarily Bo, temporarily." Bolo and I are both 5'8 but he's 190 pounds of solid muscle, and I'm only 150 of the same and to see us workout seems to be a mismatch until you see him pressing his weight and me pressing 40 pounds more than my own.

The weight room is also a dangerous area because it's small, always crowded and too far from the bubble. So even though me and Bolo are concentrating on our workout, the radar detectors are still fully operational.

Bolo gets up after his seventh set, and I take his place. I size up the bar with 2-45's and 2-35's on it, take a deep breath, and begin to rip my muscles. By the six rep the bar gets heavy and pressing it gets difficult and Bo noticing it says, "Come on gimme four more." I give him his money and sit up on the bench as my arms burn and adrenaline rushes through my bloodstream. I stand up feelin' the strength in my body begin to grow and . . . A familiar face catches my eye. I can only get a profile view—and—it's him.

I'm frozen with a mind-twisting surge of violent visions

containing every form of bodily mutilation and torture I've ever witnessed on cable. The face is of the one who sentenced me to the destruction of life as I knew it. He's the mothafucka who single handedly snatched my love from me, imprisoned me in this compound of hell, and scarred me for life. I reach down and pick up a 10-pound plate and say, "Yo Bo, hold me down." Instantly he moves into a back-up position to alert me of police or to stop an attack from behind. I move through the crowd with my mind focused on my victim like I have done several times when stalkin' my prey. My vic moves to the bench and lays down as if askin' to have his skull crushed by the steel object and let his blood fill this room like a spilled barrel of molasses. For a minute, my mind flashes back to the bloody booty bandit scene in Auburn. This must be my shit—hittin' niggas on the bench—it brings more blood.

I close in on his position completely unseen with my stealth mode, and just as I'm in bashing range, a deeper sense of revenge stops me from crackin' this nigga and killin' him. The nigga would be getting off too easy. He caused me almost two years of pain with more to come. He made Ebony and my Mother cry, and he gets off with just dying . . . no—fuck that. This nigga's gonna suffer 10 times as much as I have. I'm gonna take every thing that he loves from him like he's done to me. I want this nigga to spend every wakin' moment agonizing, and I want him to know I did all this shit to him. He'll remember my name always as I carve it into his flesh and soul, and the nigga'll suffer from the hands of *The Chef*.

I act like I was just puttin' the weight back so this muthafucka won't peep my shit. I tell Bolo our workout has to be interrupted due to this new situation, and we bag our shit and make moves to the basketball court. The bleachers are filled because of the freezing weather, but we manage to find a spot to maintain low status. The first few minutes are silent as the insane fury that was inside me begins to calm itself like a passing tornado. Then I start from the beginning of the end of life, as I once knew it. As I tell Bo the whole shit, I relive each moment, feeling the pain again, and wondering if it will ever cease to exist. The more I reveal, the more Bolo seems to bond with me. The respect, loyalty, and dedication of his Japanese side embraces my pain and makes it his own, and now, he too is willing to make a sacrifice for the cause.

Bolo has not seen the face of the victim of my vengeance, and we talk until standby for the go back is called. Bolo searches the crowd as I point the vic out—to his surprise he knows my vic. As fate would have it, Bo's cube is right next to his.

The walk back is in silence as I slip in and out of consciousness due to my thoughts of vengeance, and as always, Bo holds me down. We part and he asks, "Yo Sun you want me to handle that for you?" I can't let Bolo be a part of this yet, "Na, just watch the nigga until I come up with somethin'."

The next movement is at 1:00, and instead of the gym, I go to the library. I need to be off-guard to think and plan my next move. I sit at a table frontin' with a book. My mind is spinning uncontrollably—emotions are bouncin' back and forth—confusion, anger, pain, depression, stress, love, hate. I can't control what's goin' on in my head. I thought about my mother and how traumatic this whole shit has been for her, she's held her head and maintained for everybody. She's the only thing keepin' my family together. My little brother will never be the same, Ted and Gwen . . . I can't imagine how they feel, and Ebony—God only knows how she's able to sleep at night. I can't let this nigga get away with this; the nigga gots to pay for what he did. How can I look my peoples in the face knowing I had the chance to punish this nigga—I can't and I'm not . . . the nigga's gotta leak.

After the 4:00 count, I play my cube to concoct a scheme to put this nigga to rest. I lay in my bunk, jack in to the sultry woman of soul Anita Baker and open my mind to all possible forms of carnage. I see this nigga being stabbed up and havin' his tongue cut out so when left in a remote place to bleed to death he can't call for help. Knockin' out all his fronts, and sellin' his bitch ass to some booty bandit, chump nigga and being sold to become a sex slave for like three-four niggas. Na . . . it has to be something he'll face every day of his life. He's gotta be scarred inside and out. He's gotta taste the sweet juice of true pain; he must know anguish; he must know self torment; he must answer the call of living death. First . . . I'll become his friend so he'll trust me like a brother. Then at a moment when he's crazy happy just when he feels he's on top of the world, I'll strike like a poison pet. I'll take my revenge, finally being satisfied as I see The Chef carved into his chest and he screams in pain as his blood flows like the tears of the people who love me.

The Set Up

The next day when I see Bolo in the gym, we make moves into that hard flesh-cutting frigid mountain weather to discuss our plans 'cause the bleachers have too many ears. At first I didn't want Bolo to get involved 'cause it isn't his beef, but after I told him the whole shit, he wasn't tryin' not to be down. When me and him first met I was showin' the nigga limited love off the strength of my mans and 'em. Then they got transferred and Bolo was the only nigga I was fuckin' with. The nigga was livin' off the state, and I had more then enough to live off so—whatever I had, he had—no questions asked. So my plan included two instead of one.

The policy at facility for minor infractions is to move the niggas involved to dorms on opposite sides of the jail to limit the chances of them meeting again. Now Bolo and I are on opposite sides of the facility so we're only able to speak to each other in the gym. The only way I could be sure to be moved into Bolo's cube is if we both had a fight at the same time, but this is not as easy as it sounds. One major fact would be the officers on duty. If either of them are assholes trying to over do their job, we could be sent to the box. If they were too cool, they'd just keep the whole shit quiet. We gotta get officers who are willin' to make the call and unwilling to write shit up or box us. The plan is simple enough, but the timing is imperative. If we set shit off too far apart, we would be sent to different dorms. The weekend relief officers are our best bet.

Saturday night—8:00—movie time in every dorm, the day room is packed and ripe for the pickings. Most of these niggas been waitin' all week to have this moment of false peace. This shit right here makes our days empty and the routine is the cause of the mental death that we go through. Imagine doing the same thing day in and day out for two to 10 years; imagine how hard it can be. You know how you feel working and following the same regiment—you long for a vacation and a day off. What if you couldn't take a vacation or take a day off . . . think how you'd feel. Would the shit drive you crazy? Some of us have family on the outside or Walkmans to help us break up the monotony of the day; others have nothing and rely on HBO, SHO, or Cinemax to free them. And I'm coming to disrupt it. Definite drama.

At a quarter to eight, I place six chairs in the first and second row closest to the TV. If the chair is unoccupied long enough, someone will confiscate that spot. Only the live niggas sit in these two rows, and I know one of them will take it upon themselves to sit there until another recognized live nigga asks for it back. But if they've been there well into the movie this can be instigated into beef.

Eight forty-five—15 minutes before part one is to be executed, I walk into the day room and stand in the back to evaluate the situation. The nigga I set it on has to be well picked. Seats 1 and 2 are occupied by two Bloods. They're not a problem, but if any thing jumps off with either of them,

I'll be forced to deal with them both and they're gat bussers. If there's blood shed, we'll all end up in the box, somethin' a nigga ain't tryin' to have right now. Seat number 3—Pops he's been down 20 joints and he can hold his own but niggas know I'm live, and I'll lose points for that seemingly cowardly act. 4—Tigre, semi-live cat, will fight if backed into a corner or herbed—yeah I think I—ahh naa. The day I came in the house, he saw me step to a nigga who I thought might wanna see me so I put pressure on the nigga for some trees, so I know he'll fold. Black has the fifth—Brooklyn cat, crazy twisted but not stupid. He's got a level 7-8 phd and he's not holdin'. I think I got a winner. I approach my stage, and for the first time in awhile, my heart is racing and my stomach is filled with butterflies, I know I'm not afraid—but I'm nervous. I can't fuck this up—I can't let my peoples down— everything depends on this one moment. I stand at the edge of the row and, "Yo Black ,you gotta find another seat." Loud enough to be heard by the first three rows. My tone was borderline threatening but my face said disrespect. He looks at me as if he was computing the whole scene. Then he looks at the TV contemplating whether or not he wants to move quickly. I take advantage and say, "Nigga you don't make enough money to think about it." This shifted all the attention to us. Now, everyone knows I'm far from Bluff Daddy status and Black is a full fledged member of the playa haters club, and if either of us would back down, we would surely lose points, which means the challenge must be met. "Fuck that—NOW! I ain't gotta do a mothafuckin' thing." he says.

"Oh yeah, then you must wanna get tested. I'll be in the

bathroom nigga; don't talk about it, be about it." The show-ers are always the designated fight zone because the officers don't enter it on their routine rounds. But once an audi-ence forms to witness the event, I know the C.O. will make it his business to check the scene. I make my way to the bathroom knowing I have at least three minutes before Black's phd supersedes his intellect. On my way I tell a lame to hold me down as I regulate. The lame wastes no time informing the rest of the dorm about the fight causing everyone to blow the spot because two well-recognized, live niggas will definitely be an interesting bout.

A small group of spectators follows Black into his arena of failure, and this will be a critical moment for me if I want to succeed. As Black presents himself, I can sense the con-fusion and fear in his heart. I've always tried to maintain low status and only unleash my fury when necessary and this new shit is straight up off the rocker. Black knows my knuckle game is up to par, and he really didn't want to test my skills but his phd wouldn't allow him to back down first. So I give him the opportunity to talk his way out of this not, because I didn't want to fight, but to give the officer enough time to realize something is going on.

I initiated the lip professing with, "I'm sayin' Son, you just gonna disrespect me like I ain't nobody right?"

"Na Dog, you just came at me on some bullshit so I said fuck it, if you wanna take it there, then what ever."

"So what was all that hesitation about when I told you to give me my seat back?"

"First of all, muthafuckas don't tell me to do shit and

second of all-" As I stood with my back to the wall Black stood in front of me and behind him is the entrance where the officer's face pops up in the small window in the center of it. Swiftly I hit Black with a light blow to the jaw, a blow which he has seen a few others fall victim to and be stretched out. This will cause him to think about my intentions and later not be upset but thankful that there was no malice behind the action.

Quickly the C.O. steps into the bathroom, "All right that's enough Davis, pack it up and be at the bubble. Ross, you come with me." So far so good, I make moves to my cube but not anxiously, it might seem like I set this whole shit up. You know what though these punk-ass country bumpkins ain't smart enough to peep my shit . . . Bolo . . . I hope he did his job. Hell yeah he did, Bolo's the only nigga who I've trusted since I've been down. The Japenese are crazy loyal and respect is something that's been a tradition, "L dorm requesting u.a.m., L dorm requesting a u.a.m." Unauthorized move. That's what they call an in-facility move that they want to keep quiet from the administration.

The C.O. unlocks the steel double reinforced door and tells me I'm headed G dorm. I creep outside with two clear garbage bags filled with my property. The night is still crisp and calm. The compound's buildings are only three stories high so there's no obstacles to prevent the moon's glowing shine from lacing my soul. During the day, these walkways flow like rivers of agony and anguish disguised by rage and fury. But right now, it's quiet and serene, like . . . I'm not in jail. Damn—it's a hell of a feeling.

As I make my way through the walkways of hell, I see another warrior of death. The extremely bright florescent lights distort his facial features, but he's still in green. He's still a threat, he's . . . he's familiar. I was so caught up in this peaceful scene that I forgot the reason why I was on this mission. But my man Bolo didn't forget. We both know we're being watched and any display may put a nigga on suspect mode. We don't even speak. For a brief moment, the moon's rays clash with the floodlights illuminating one spot in this endless concrete jungle. In that brief moment as we pass in that simple blink of an eye, we seal the sacred covenant that is now our friendship.

It's 9:15 p.m. as I begin to unpack and set up shop in my new drop zone. Each item is placed strategically 'cause each move I make is now done with the conscious precision; my mission won't fail. This nigga must answer of his crimes— he will pay.

I place photos sent by my momz and my peoples in plain view so my victim will want to discuss the beauty of my girl and where they were taken. Next—all the magazines I got, I put on top of my small locker, again to lure him into a conversation. And finally my tapes, all these items are a connection to the outside world, which is what every nigga in here will die for, and can't live without. I know this nigga is a typical jail nigga, crazy grimy, manipulative, and sneaky. Once he sees all the shit I got, which we all need to survive, he'll make it his business to try to live off me. And you know what, I'll just make myself available for the setup; thereby, causing the nigga to be totally unaware of the shit

I'm about to lay down. 9:45 count time, I sit on the bed and watch as each cube is filled, then I see him . . . My heart starts pounding as a fiery rush fills my body, my mind, and soul. I spin into a cyclone of hate, my jaw locks, and my fist tightens as if to crush the bones in my own hand. I look away so my eyes won't give away my plan. The C.O. comes past and it's only minutes before he yells, "Counts clear."

I lay in silence using the Queen of finesse Sade to calm the raging demon that distorts my mind. I try to go over my plan hopin' that thinking about it will give me the calm cool collectiveness I'll need to pull this shit off. This muthafucka took me from my people without even thinking, then he tried to kill me. Na, fuck the bullshit. I'm takin' this nigga out tonight—No! No! I gotta chill and stick to the plan. I can't let my emotions interrupt my goal. I gotta stay on point—gotta maintain.

On the count, I peeped him takin' inventory of my shit, just what I wanted him to do. The nigga don't even know he's fallin' right into my hands. By tomorrow, he'll be standin' at the divider askin' for somethin. Because niggas spend all day together, the shit I'ma lay down won't take too long. The plan is simple and this nigga's got hunger pains written all over his face, so he can't help but to be greedy, and I'm about to monopolize on it.

10:00, lights out in the dorm. Again I'm alone with my thoughts, and I try to ease the ball of rage that has begun to flow and build momentum like the furry of an avalanche. Yet my reflections betray me, like I've said, the only thing that can somewhat ease the gut wrenching torment of day-to-day life is the beauty of the outside world. The beauty of the ones you love, their scent, their smile, even their anger is welcomed because laughter always follows when they are true friends. These insights of love are also what feeds the turbulent beast of ravaging annihilation that has been unleashed in this correctional system. A beast that becomes impatient when it smells a vic, a vic that is unaware of his own demise. A vic that doesn't know he's sleeping next to the enemy.

$ $ $ $ $

Days pass and every night now Red is at the divider talkin' bullshit about Harlem like I give a fuck about N.Y. He thinks he's gonna put me down on his team so he can juice me. Good,'cause I got a trick for his ass.

Friday night in G dorm, movie night again, like about 7:00 niggas start puttin' their chairs in their spots and makin' dinner, rollin' trees or drinkin' hooch. Tonight is a hooch night. Some nigga got some grapefruit juice from the mess hall and made two jugs and one of them belonged to Red, which meant this would be a perfect time for me to owe him.

"Yo Chef you got a jug?"

"Yeah, why?"

"I got somethin' for you." He slides off and comes back and hits me off. I take it realizing this is the trap set by the hunter, but he doesn't know he has become the hunted. I open my mouth and let the fermented jailhouse special fill my throat with its potency. This shit stinks but it does its job; it's a temporary escape from the mental hell. It takes

me beyond this realm of hate and destruction, and it puts me a step closer to completing my mission. Damn right, I'm gonna drink this nasty shit, whatever it takes to ease the pain of fuckin' with this nigga. But back to the thick shit, I decide to give him an opportunity to dig himself deeper into a hole, "Yo I got somethin' to blaze."

"I'm good I got stogies."

"Na, nigga I got somethin' to BLAZE."

"Say word."

"Word."

"Aiight, let me know when you ready."

"No doubt." Clown ass nigga, he' so fuckin' slimy and greedy, he didn't even peep how I flipped his shit right back on him. Stupid muthafucka.

Later that night, me and Red get twisted and I know I got this nigga right where I want him. The funny shit is he don't even remember me, all this time I stand in his face and he don't even fuckin' remember me. Yeah, I'm here to punish his bitch ass—chill don't think about it gotta stay focused. Yo, I don't even know how I'm maintainin' right now. This shit should be drivin' me crazy, but fuck it—tend to business.

7:15 a.m. I'm up and on my way to chow. I usually don't fuck with this jail food but I gotta get a kite to Bo. I don't trust anyone else so it's gotta be hand delivered.

The walk to chow is a total drain on my spirit. Every inmate in this Devil's paradise is starvin' for the loving energy of the outside would. Niggas is like energy magnets but half of them are twisted so they're like parasites, and just walking through this sea of green is a fight. I enter the mess hall as one of the four-at-a-time niggas lookin' for the brolic little Japanese nigga. Bolo exits the kitchen with a pitcher of water and a hand towel. He's got table tops. Perfect, now my shit is gonna come off. The line drags along and I pick up a tray and grab the bullshit breakfast and sit where I'm told. Within minutes, Bolo heads over to my table, and as he approaches, I remove a small piece of folded paper from my pocket. I place it on the table out of sight of the punk ass c.o.'s and Bolo picks it up as he cleans off the table, mission accomplished. In my kite, I let my man know the deal and what I need from him. This next step is a straight up multidimensional move.

Sunday, v.i. day for me, Ebony's comes alone. My mother came with her the last two weekends. I can't wait to tell her—no I can't. I want to but she won't understand. She won't understand the hate I have for him. She'll probably try to talk me out of it.

I start my visit routine like a few other cats in the dorm. I try to find shit to do 'cause I woke up too early—now I'm nervous—the clock is ticking and my mind is fuckin' with me. What I'ma do if she don't come, I need that package— I'ma call—it's too fuckin' early, phones ain't even on yet. I throw the headphones on and relax my shit out. "60 bed, on the visit." Showtime, Eb brought a surprise for the nigga who held me down when I needed, a nigga I broke bread with. I make my way across the walkways in silence because I have to prepare myself for a family visit. I can't let Ebony see the scars this place has left on my mind, body and soul.

I can't let her know about this new constant pain I endure by being right next to the nigga who fucked our lives up.

I absorb the sun's early morning rays and use its power to camouflage my pain and—in the distance I see my man—Bolo. He's in a hurry, the nigga's still buttonin' his shirt,

"What up Sun, who came to check you."

"I don't know, my girl ain't write me and say she was comin'. I ain't got a letter from her in like three months."

"Maybe she came to surprise you."

"Na, she ain't got the dough for that. Between her school bills plus the regular shit—shit is real tight. She ain't got no kids but it's still hard."

"True. At least you got a v.i."

"Word. It really don't matter who it is."

We enter the area where we get frisked before hittin' the v.i. room and Bo's crazy nervous. He's excited. This is the first time I've seen him like this. Now I know what I look like to other niggas when I'm on a v.i. After a brief pat down, we enter through the door that brings us to the paradise in our burning hell. This visiting room allows men who are in a war for their soul, to see the families who long for and miss their presence. For eight hours, we pretend we're not torn apart. We pretend we don't cry after lights out. We act as if we're all right with leaving when it's over.

Ebony and Bolo's girl Amy are at two tables that are side by side. Me and Bo shine because we needed to see our loves; the shit we're about to go through is fuckin' with us. We embrace our loves with a grip that is uncontrollable when you're in love, we say I miss you with our faces tucked deep within their necks. Bolo sits and, "Why you ain't tell me you was comin'?"

"It was a surprise."

"Where'd you get the money for the ticket?"

"I didn't take the bus, Ebony gave me a ride. Von wanted to give you somethin' and here I am." And she places her hands on his face because she misses the warmth of his soul. And without question, she kisses him once because she loves him, once because he's a beautiful man, and once because he brings happiness to her life. For a moment Bolo is trapped deep within the love she gives him then he turns to me and, "Yo . . ." and his look is one of much honor and respect, "I'm yo nigga for life." And with equal homage to his oath, "No question." Then as quickly as he makes that bond, we return to where our minds should be—our girls.

Bolo and Amy are in full visit mode kissing every two minutes and takin' crazy pictures. Me and Eb's visit is more routine now. The home updates and the I love yous and miss yous are no more. Now it's about straight up survival. We both need these visits. they're the only thing that helps us to keep our sanity. We've long passed the grieving stage. it's just a matter of waiting this storm out. All we can do for each other now is be there when the other person gets weak or scared—all we can do is be there for each other. No question Ebony feels my pain as I feel hers—but can she feel the warmth and compassion I felt when Bolo saw his girl. I wonder if she can sense the feelings I'm trying to hide. I can't let niggas see the weaker side of me—that's certain death.

Ebony's telling me about something that happened at

her job. She has to keep talking to keep herself from cryin'
so I let her ramble as long as she needs. I'm tryin' to listen,
but this shit with Red is fuckin' with me, day and night, I'm
thinkin' about my revenge. Every waking moment is
focused on the outcome of my plan. I want to tell her what's
goin' on. I wanna talk to somebody about the shit that's
about to jump off. I'm not used to this dolo shit, I always
talked to Eb or my momz, but this thing is all on me. I'm all
on my own on this one. My peoples ain't gonna understand
this twisted shit. They not gonna be able to see this is necessary. No way in the world can I let this nigga get away.

Me and Bolo are the last ones to leave the floor and the
last ones to hit the package room. I told Eb to get the same
thing for him that she gets for me, so as we part at the fork
in the road heavy with two bags apiece, "Yo Chef—I mean
Von, I'm for real Dog—Ya nigga for life."

"And I'm yours kid."

Back at my cube, I start putting my stuff away when Red
slithers through, *"Yo what up cuzin' visit was aiight?"*

"No doubt." And I toss an extra large bag of Doritos and
a can of Crystal Light lemonade on his bed. He looks at me
and, *"Oh word. Good lookin'."*

"Aiight."

"Yo, you graduated from high school?"

"Yeah."

*"Yo, do me a favor . . . I'm sayin' . . . you think you could
help me write this letter to my girl?"* Mmm, the shit done
jumped up a couple of notches, "No doubt, just let me know
when you're ready."

"Aiight—good lookin'."

This new shit has sped up my plan, Red wants me to write his girl which means he trusts me enough to let me see his weaker side, the side that shows his girl love. But I'ma make sure the noose around his neck is even tighter.

A couple of days after the v.i., I wake up to the dark skies of my hell, but today is special, today is the day when shit thickens and takes hold of Red. That letter to Bolo was to set up my plan and now it's time to make it happen.

Me and Red join the sea of green that fills the walkways and I'm not as swift as I once was. I just gotta—this plan has gotta work—I can't let my people down I hope this nigga Bolo—chill kid, slow down, shit'll fall apart if you don't relax. I gotta maintain. I can't let Red know somethin's about to jump off. We enter the gym, sign in, hit the weight room, and I see Bolo settin' up with some lame young nigga—the decoy. I slide over and claim the bench next to them, not acknowledging or making eye contact with either of them. Niggas start getting their workout on and I pick up two 20's and, "I'ma get some 40's."

"Aiight." I hit the rack and lay in the cut—it's Bolo's turn. I look over my shoulder and see Bolo talkin' to Red, I don't know what Bo said to him but the shit worked. Red stands up and I look away; he's playin' right into it. Seconds later, I make my move. I head for the scene praying my man sticks to the plan. I step in between them and hit my man with a simple six move hand to hand combination, a combination he taught me when we first met, a combination we

practiced. A simple combination that can make a nigga think we're shootin' the crazy five. And Red'll think I stepped up for him and then I'll have his loyalty and he'll owe me. The bootleg fight scene we laid down is quick quiet and right on point. I ain't tryin' to cause a commotion and bring attention to us, with the swiftness Red pulls me away and, *"Maintain nigga, police is watchin'."* Yeah—I scoop up my wears and hit Bolo with the ice face. Bolo knows that's the good lookin'.

Back in the bleachers, "Yo Sun what was all that 'bout?"

"I don't know, money started talkin' some dumb shit like he wanted it. I was 'bout to bring it to him but you came through. Good lookin'."

"It's all good."

"Yo what was all that karate shit?"

"I peeped money a couple of months ago doin' his little work out and if you and him was to go toe, to toe he might've put it on you 'cause you ain't know he had that karate shit locked down. So I did my little shit. On the real—if you ain't step in he would've reacted me 'cause my shit is amateur statues compared to him."

"Aiight." Yeah, this muthafucka doesn't even realize I can see his mind workin'. He's flippin' the scene over. He knows he owes me, but how can he use it to get over, slimy muthafucka. My man Bolo did his thing right. He came through when I needed him. Niggas for life.

Red has been at my divider on a reg and the shit's so thick sometimes I forget I'm frontin'.

Four thirty-after the count, every nigga in the dorm is at the bubble—mail call. I lay back 'cause I ain't tryin' to be around all the lames, plus Eb doesn't write like she used to so I don't look for letters any more. But Red always hopes to be blessed, and today, *"Yo Sun my girl just sent me a kite, can you read it for me?"* Damn—the niggas like 26 and he can't read? It's fucked up—but I don't give a fuck. I'm still gonna get his ass. "No doubt." I see the same excitement in his face that I was in Bo's. I should blast his ass right now— fuckin' illiterate bastard, punk muthafucka—not yet. I crack the thick envelope and realize, "Yo there's two letters in here." The first looks like a child's handwriting, *"That's my son, read that one first."*

Dear Daddy,
I hope you are doing fine in the army. I'm doing good in school. My teacher says I can skip a grade if I keep good grades. Mommy is still mad at you. But I don' t get mad because I remember our secret. Myra said to tell you she loves you and we want you to come home soon.
Love always, your
son Tyriq

Red's face speaks the words he can't express or accept in here. *"I can't have him knowin' I'm locked up, so I'm in the army. But I think I'ma tell him the truth. . . . Read the other one."*

Dear Red,

I hope this letter will bring brightness to your day as you have done in mine.

Pa, I'm not going to waste this letter beefing at you for something you know you were wrong for doing. You fucked up big time and we're both fucked up because of it.

Now that I've got that out the way, you really need to write me and let me know where you are so I can come see you. I really miss you Pa. I'm not going to write a long letter because I'm starting to cry already. Just let me know if you're alive please. I love you Pa. Yo tengo mi amour.

Myra

"What's the deal Red? Your girl is tryin' to see you and you hidin'? What's up, you gotta long bid or somethin'?" He snatches the letters and says, "*Na, I just ain't ready to see them. . . I gotta get my head right first.*"

"What? Yo what kinda shit could stop you from getting love from your peoples?"

"*Sun, I'm tryin' to better myself. I wanna learn how to read and write. I gotta cut out all that stick-up shit. A nigga needs to think about his kid and this chic who loves me. On the real Sun, ain't nothin' left in them streets for me. What they got, I don't need no more.*"

"Aiight. I hear you." But you still gotta pay for the shit you done in the past.

Dark Water

I sit up on the edge of the bed—it's like 2:00. I know

'cause this nigga Chef is up. Every time I wake up 'cause some shit is on my mind, this nigga is up. Either we be havin' problems at the same time or he's always up. I ain't worried though, the nigga's aiight—you know—real good peoples. He's the only nigga in here that don't make me nervous.

I lay back down tryin' to go back to sleep but I can't. I might get a visit today. It's up in the air 'cause it's some shysty shit behind it.

Storm

2:00 a.m., New York is in full dark side mode, as the inmates sleep and the day is at rest. One boy prepares for a trip. Little eight year old Tyriq wakes to an alarm clock, he slides out the bed and begins a routine reserved to school days. Today is Saturday and there isn't school and –ring— ring. Tyriq runs to the phone and, "Hello."

"Tyriq "

"Yes who's this?"

"It's Storm. I'm a friend of your father. I'm supposed to pick you up and take you somewhere."

"What are you supposed to say to me to let me know I'm supposed to go with you."

"Keep it on the down low."

"O.K."

"Be downstairs at 2:30. I'm gonna be in a red car and I'ma have on a black hat."

"Red car black hat. Got it."

"Aiight one."

Tyriq moves through the empty two bedroom freely

'cause his momz ain't home again. Fridays she bounces out and doesn't come home until morning, so my little man Tyriq is used to being alone. He makes himself a bowl of cereal after getting dressed, then the Cartoon Network until 2:25.

Tyriq enters the dark side as merely a traveler the destruction and temptations don't interest him yet. The doorway that is the exit to his world and entrance to the dark waters swings open and the demons that flow through this river smell the purity of an innocent soul. They send out the energy that would entangle his mind like a web of death, but he chants four words that, unknown to him, will save his life for today, "Red car, black hat." He whispers to himself. "Come on Tyriq we gotta move," Tyriq hadn't fully exposed himself to the dark waters when the voice called out to him and his heart says don't trust the voice. He tackles each step slowly knowing he's moving on to dangerous ground. The closer he gets, the more the inside of the car is exposed and now another person begins to appear. A lady, "Myra!" Tyriq jumps off the last four steps and jets to the back door, pops it and hops in—safety at last.

3:00 a.m., 59th and Columbus Circle is alive with not dark side dwellers but with day invaders. Myra joins the line of women as old as 50 and as young as 18, some with infants strapped to their chests and children at their legs; others have children and bags of necessities for their sons, husbands, uncles, and baby's fathers. Every weekend, these busloads of women travel, five to eight hours. Some of them even make overnight trips to visit the ones they love who have been taken hostage by the D.O.C. This, on top of

having to wake up at midnight in order to have themselves
and their children ready and then not getting home until 10-
11:00 at night because of the ride back. These women have
to pretend it doesn't hurt to be searched, locked behind a
wall or gate and see their loved ones for a mere eight hours.

Myra and Tyriq take their places in the visiting room
waiting to see the man they both love, and whom they
haven't seen in almost two years. Red's been on some bullshit. He's been sending them letters but never giving them
any visiting information. You do whatever you gotta do to
survive, no matter whose feelings are hurt.

Red enters the room he hasn't seen since his last bid,
and for the first time in years, the nigga is happy.

This nigga Red goes on the dance floor today, so I slide
to the gym to see my man Bolo to check his status and
update him. I also need to bless him one more time for
being my man, so I call Eb from the gym and have her hit
Amy on the three-way for Bo. I know he doesn't get to talk
to her because she can't afford it, but I know a nigga needs
it. For 25 minutes, my man has happiness and I give him his
space to rock. Then in the solitude of the weekend yard,
"Yo Von, my girl told me some football player lookin' cat
with a baby face came by her job and gave her some money
for me and her."

"Big Ted. His girl calls him Teddy Bear."

"Yo nigga, I ain't never—"

"I'm sayin' don't be thankin' me for some shit I'm supposed to do. I take care of niggas who take care of me."

"You don't have to keep doin' shit for me, that one v.i. was enough."

"I'm sayin' that's just for the this last shit-"

"Yo you my man I don't want you to be payin' me off for some shit I wanna do."

"You right it ain't like you work for me or somethin'. Aiight no more payoffs. But I am gonna have Eb bring your girl up every once in awhile, aiight?"

"No doubt."

When I get back to the dorm, Red is already there and he starts tellin' me about the v.i. and, *"I ain't tryin' to go back to the same life I was livin'. I got a son who's smart as a muthafucka and a girl who'll do anything for me. I can't ever jeopardize their lives with some bullshit. I got one more year left on this violation, and I'ma see if I can get work release so I can come home to some shit that can help me get my shit together. I ain't never had a job in my life, and on the real, a nigga needs to do somethin' to get right."*

"I hear you kid, do what you gotta do, you know. Tell your counselor the same shit you just told me and she might set your shit up for you."

"I hope so cuzin'. It's time for a nigga to make a serious change." I listen to this nigga tell me all this extra shit and it begins to burn a hole in my chest. I don't give a fuck about him changin'. He can't escape his past. He can't forget and move on—who the fuck he think he is? No redemption for the lives he's taken, no forgiveness for the destruction he's caused—no—only punishment—only my revenge.

COME INTO THE LIGHT

Night falls on the facility. Every nigga in here falls back on the things that keep the pain away. Yet the tears still fall because we're alone, and the suffering and the mental torture we endure is a fight for even the strongest willed.

I sit in my cube in darkness watching this nigga Red by the moonlight. He's asleep with the pictures from his visit in his hand. The nigga been lookin' at them shits all day and smilin' like shit is all good and sweet. Fuckin' punk, I'm tired of this nigga—I can't take it anymore. I remove the metallic prison style dagger from its hiding place and slide to all fours with it in my mouth—full navy SEAL assassin style. The chest high divider gives me the cover I need, and my water moccasin slither is at it's best. I maneuver around his barrier in silence and creep into his cube totally unseen. I rest at the edge of the bed like a gargoyle on a castle and watch the super thug breathe. I watch his chest rise and lower and the demon that has been caged for too long emerges with pride and excitement. I remove my weapon ready to christen it with the blood of the bitch-ass nigga

219

who made me the monster that I am. I look at his face, hating every inch of his existence with the deepest inner light that is my soul. I rise slowly—dagger in hand. I double grip it because I'm not gonna scar him—he's gonna die tonight—he's gonna die on this, the best day of his worthless life. His blood is gonna spill and as the life slips out of his body, I'm gonna look deep into the eyes and take back all that he has taken from me. I'm gonna relish in the cesspool of hate that was his life and— . . . and . . . oh shit I can't bre—.

Suddenly my breath becomes short and is cut—I feel like the air is being removed from body. I drop down to the crouch and retrace my steps barely—I fall on my bunk in agony and flashes of Ebony—my Mother—my brothers— Ted, Gwen—the barbershop—the day that I called the greatest of my life hits me like a lightning bolt. What—why . . . tears fill my eyes and –what am I doing. . . I almost killed somebody. Oh my God, what happened to me, what have I become. I'm a monster—God I'm sorry, what happened to my life—I almost killed a man. I'm a monster. I get up and fall to my knees, look to the heavens and silently say, God please help me, I've become everything my mother fought to keep me from. How could I cause so much bloodshed and pain—I've hurt people for enjoyment—I cut men who did nothing to me—and I almost killed this man. Here he is regretting every thing he's ever done and tryin' to change for his son and I was going to take his life. What happened to me God? Please help me, I don't wanna be like this anymore—I don't want to hate I—*Blackout.*

I'm awakened by the warmth of the sun's rays on my face, I try to sit up and it's a task so I just lay—eyes opened and focused out the window. The sky is clear and the clouds dance in front of the sun like children on the first day of summer. I feel like I just woke up from a nightmare. My clothes and sheets are damp with sweat and I remember why. That shit that happened last night was . . . I guess . . . a spiritual awakening. It was like God gave my true spirit the power to fight the demon that took over my body. It was like an exorcism by the hand of God. I muster up enough energy to slide off the bed to my knees and, "God please forgive me for all the harm I caused and help me to become the person I once was. Please help me help myself. Help me find the strength I need to fight all the hate in my heart and around me." Just as I complete my thought, Red comes to my cube, *"Yo Chef—yo cuzin', you aiight?"* I look up at him and . . . the hate is gone. I don't feel the beast anymore. My heart isn't racing, and I'm not filled with the gut wrenching fury. My mind doesn't race along the tracks of mutilation and carnage. The demon is gone. "Yeah I'm good—just prayin'."

"Yo, say a prayer for me too. I'm about to send in this work release application. I got one for you too. I figure you got a good chance of getting accepted too. If a niggas one year to the board and your record ain't too bad, they usually take you." I stand up still weak and . . . Red helps me up. A calming peace comes over me and as I look in his eyes, I see a different person—the monster who shot me that day isn't there—oh shit—oops, sorry God. The almighty has stepped in and regulated. God don't play no games.

Me and Red fill out the short one-page application before I hop in the shower and try to wash away all that hate. All the hate that I kept inside and unleashed on any and everyone for two years.

The revelation that cleared my mind was something I could not keep to myself, so I had to make a phone call. Eb is strong but she can't help with this, "Ma?"

"Yeah baby how you doin'?"

"Better."

"You all right baby—did somethin' happen?"

"If only you knew."

"Talk to me Von, what's wrong?" I fill her in on the nights events and why and a lot of the things that happened since the Island. And the silence that plagues the phone is for my mother's own sanity. "Well honey, whatever you had to do to survive on Rikers Island was necessary. I told you God doesn't put people in any situation they can't handle. And . . . everyone in life goes through a test to move them to the next level of life, and you have just gone through one of the hardest test I can imagine. You were put into a pit of hell fire, and when you had to make the choice between the Devil's way and God's way, you made the right decision, you did some bad things, yes, but when given the choice to cross the line of no return you didn't. You took the test of life and passed. Whenever you make a mistake, you're supposed to learn from it so all the things you did that you felt were mistakes. See what they taught you then, hold on to the lesson and dump the rest and move on with your life.

You and Eb only have a bright future ahead of you, if you both can get pass this thing you're in. So remember that. And you said the guy who put you in this situation showed you a way to get out of it the day after you spared his life. That's a sign if I ever saw one. Here you were ready to kill him and if you did, you might've got caught and given more years, but you didn't and God has blessed you with a way out. He's telling you the test is over and you can go home. Fill those papers out and pray, and go back to the way you were when you were happy—remember those days. Envision yourself home doing all the things you love to do. If you convince yourself—if you truly believe you can come home, you will. For a long time Von, you never could imagine going home because you thought these people could keep you forever. But do you see now that there is a power greater than them—do you see God is the only one who has the power to free you?

Every night you should pray to come home and thank God you're not dead and that you have people who love you and who'll support you. This is the end baby and before you know it, you and Ebony will be coming over for Sunday dinner."

"Yeah—the phone's about to cut off—"

"O.K. remember what I said baby, stay strong. We'll be praying for that work release for you too. We love you."

"I love y'all too—bye."

The words my mother spoke make sense of this situation and for the first time I recognize and acknowledge the power of God.

A week after Red sent our papers in, we're in front of a three-man committee and being intrested. I was first, "So Mr. Davis, according to your record, you were convicted of gun possession. You wanna tell us about it?" Not really. "Well it's really simple. I was being robbed in front of my building and I fought off the guy—he shot me, I got the gun away from him and shot back but he got away. Since my prints were the only ones they were able to get off the gun, it was automatically mine. Cut and dry. I copped out on the advice of a crappie lawyer and here I sit in front of you hoping this nightmare will end soon."

"And I also see you spent some time in the box. Another injustice?"

"Not really. Umm, I was mistakenly sent to Auburn— some kind of classification mix up. And umm—how can I put this. Well I caught the eye of someone who was twice my size and I had to physically decline his offer for a relationship, if you know what I mean."

"I see, well Mr. Davis, we usually don't even consider people with your kind of charge but we'll at least discuss it and give you a response in the next couple of days. O.K."

"Thank you."

"Send in the next person please." I slide out feeling like—I'm not going to think about it. It's in God's hands. "Red—you up."

The next four days I find myself standing in front of the bubble lookin' for the response letter, praying to be given a chance to once again taste freedom. And finally, "60 bed Davis." I snatch the stapled envelope knowing it's in-house mail and head for my cube. I sit on the bed and say a silent one before reading it.

Davis, Devon, 99A6170.
This letter is to notify you that you have been accepted to the work release program.

Damn . . . I can't believe it. My stomach flutters like an adolescent cat on his first date and all I can say is, "Thank you God." A tear swells in my eye and before it can call on its friends I head for the phones.

"Yo Eb, call my mother on the three way, she's probably still at her office."

"O.K. hold on."

"Evelyn Davis."

"Ma."

"Von? How-" says Ma.

"Eb's on the phone too."

"Hi Ebony." Says Ma.

"Hello Ms. Evelyn." Says Eb.

"O.K. So what's goin' on?" says Ma.

"Listen, I'm about to tell you both somethin' and I need you to just listen . . . The whole time I was goin' through this bid y'all two have been the only ones to support me. Ebony, I can't begin to thank you for stickin' by me. And Ma, I see how these other mothers do some of these guys, and I know I don't say it enough but I really do appreciate what you've done." Slowly the tears fall, "I love y'all to death . . .and . . . I would do anything for you both. I know it's been hard on you both but . . . it's almost over—I got accepted to work release."

"Oh my God—Von oh my God thank you I'm gonna cry—oh thank you." Says Eb.

"Thank you God. It's finally over—my baby is coming home," says Ma.

"I don't know when but it should be soon so-"

"O.K. This is it. See I told you both, stay true to God and he'll bless you. All right let's get ready for your home-comin'." Says Ma.

"I'll call ya'll when I get some more information."

Back at my cube, I play like everything is everything. I ain't tryin to let anybody know what's up until I know I'm out.

That night I went to bed early and slept all night—no 4am wake-up—no restless nightmares, just peaceful sleep.

The next afternoon after the count, "60 bed Davis, pack it up, you on the draft." What! Oh shit. Sorry God. The state needs to put another nigga through this mental torture so it's time for me to go. They don't waste any time filling the bed space—one out, one in—keep the doors of hell swinging.

After I drop my bags off at the draft office, I rock the jack and call as many people as I can. Me and Ebony stay on the phone from like 6 to 9, I couldn't stop her from run-nin' her mouth, she was goin' on and on about what we were gonna do the first day I get home. And the second day and the third and the fourth then the month. It made me feel good to hear the happiness in her voice. I almost forgot what it sounded like. The whole time she was talking, I could envision her facial expressions in my mind, her smile her laugh, her love. I can't believe it's over. When I finally get off the phone, Red is waiting at my cube.

"So you outta here, it'll be my turn soon, I got my approval today. And on the real, I'm ready to end all the bullshit in my life. I ain't tryin' to be runnin' wild anymore. I got a little dough stashed away and I'ma try to get my parole switched down to VA. My little brother's down there. He got a house 'n shit so me and Myra an my son can stay with him. I think she'll be with it. She said she'd think about it again. When I first asked her, she was with it then I fucked around and got knocked and she was a little noid. But . . ."

"You be treatin' her right?"

"Yeah—I'm sayin' I was on some bullshit sometimes but all in all it was aiight."

"You wish you could change some of the shit you did?"[1]

"Not really 'cause I did what I had to do to live—you know—I had to feed my seed."

Then the nigga gets silent for a minute and, *"But there was one time—I used to do stick ups and one night I wild out and tried to get this nigga. Money fought a nigga for the heat and everything and he caught one in the gut. I'm sayin', at the time I was on some professional shit and to do some petty shit like that . . . I felt like I straight up violated the nigga 'cause his status was equal to mine. I don't know if the nigga died or not—I hope he didn't—he was a strong nigga, you know."* God is giving me one last test. I can help him ease this mental beef right here, right now, or do I let him torture himself with grief.

"Yo cuzin'—the nigga lived."

"What? How you know?" I lift up my shirt and show him the scar that curses my body and, "You shot me on Riverside that night kid." He looks at my eyes like he's reliving that night again, searching for a sign that I might be lying. *"How—why you—why you ain't get me back?"*

"Don't get it twisted, I was gonna do you in, but the night I was gonna do it—I realized I couldn't. I didn't wanna be a killer. For real, God helped me forgive a nigga—it just wasn't worth it."

"Damn kid, you is a strong nigga. Yo, I can't fuckin' believe I'm standin' here talkin' to you like I ain't shoot you."

"Yo, just accept it-"

"You could've killed me anytime you wanted but you didn't."

"Yo I told you God had somethin' to do with it."

"Damn . . . I guess I owe you one—"

"Na cuzin', you owe God and pay Him back by goin' home and doin' the right thing."

The End of this part of their life

Ghetto Interpreter

For some of you what you are about to be exposed to needs some clarifying. So here is a 'Ghetto interpreter.'

Scomas- Another name for marijuana

Blower- Gun

Dime Piece- A beautiful woman, perfect ten, hence dime.

Knock off- Have sex

Trooper- One who stays with someone during a trying time. One who is strong in a stressful situation.

Bid- Prison sentence

Flippin'- Arguing with someone or about something

Chicken head- A woman of low moral standings; a low class woman of any social status.

Jux- robbery

Big 8th- Another name for package of cocaine

Pedico- Cocaine

Hammer- Gun

White Horse- Cocaine habit, as in riding the white horse.

Gassed- Convincing someone of something. Gassed up to do or say . . .

Brick- A kilo of cocaine

Peel his cap back- To murder, to have skin of head peeled back by coroner.

PHD-   Playa Hata Degree

Big faces-Term to refer to the new bills with larger faces.

187-   Police code for homicide

Tim's-   Short for Timberland

Jew-els-   Reference to jewelry or can be used to refer to valuable information given.

Venom-   Extremely convincing words, the extreme of charisma. Venom can be in negative way.

Hit in head-To give someone something to think about.

Agy-   Aggravated

E.P-   Episode, usually used to refer to sexual activity. Swinging an Ep

Love-   Used in referring to showing one love, non verbal expression of this.

O.T-   Old timer

Land of the eternal shine- Harlem

Gat-   Refers to a gun. In jail setting used to describe razor or other weapon.

Slide off- To leave

Heat- Gun

Godfather- When used I reference to marijuana describes a cigar that has tobacco removed with out cutting paper and stuffed with marijuana.

Shines- Jewelry

Blasted- To be shot or cut

Jacked- To be robbed, or have something taken as in to have your heart jacked by love

Bullpen Therapy-Term used when inmates are left in holding cells for several hours, minimum of 6.

Joints- Used in the place of to describe places or things. That's my joint, who's joint is this, where's the joint at.

The jack- Telephone

Cheek- Prison term used to describe when one is placing something in anal cavity.

Dutch- Cigar used to roll blunts.

Dolo- Alone

Banger- Razor

The Turtles- Riot squad on Rikers Island

Jig- To stab

Dragon Tamer- Something used to control bad breathe.

Hot Spot- Popular club

Hatas- Ones who are jealous of people for having what they don't or are able to do what they cannot.

Shooting the five- Having a fight.

ORDER FORM

Order additional copies of *UPSTREAM PUBLICATIONS* bestselling titles.

Name:_____

Company _____

Address: _____

_____

City: _____ State_____ Zip_____

Phone: (_____)_____ Fax: (_____)_____

E-mail: _____

Credit Card:☐Visa ☐ MC ☐ Amex ☐Discover

Number _____

Exp Date: _____Signature: _____

QTY	DESCRIPTION	PRICE	TOTAL
1.			
2.			
3.			
4.			
5.			
6.			

SHIPPING INFORMATION		
Ground	one book	$ 4.50
each additional book		$ 1.25

Subtotal _____

shipping _____

8.5 % tax (NY, NJ) _____

Total _____

Make checks or money orders payable to
A&B Books
1000 Atlantic Avenue
Brooklyn, New York 11238

Books can also be purchased from online booksellers

call (718) 783-7808